PUFFIN BOOKS

BROTHER WULF

WULF'S
WAR

Also available by Joseph Delaney

THE SPOOK'S SERIES
The Spook's Apprentice
The Spook's Curse
The Spook's Secret
The Spook's Battle
The Spook's Mistake
The Spook's Sacrifice
The Spook's Nightmare
The Spook's Destiny
I Am Grimalkin
The Spook's Blood
Slither's Tale
Alice
The Spook's Revenge

The Spook's Stories: Witches
The Spook's Bestiary

The Seventh Apprentice
A New Darkness
The Dark Army
Dark Assassin

ARENA 13 SERIES
Arena 13
The Prey
The Warrior

ABERRATIONS SERIES
The Beast Awakens
The Witch's Warning

BROTHER WULF SERIES
Brother Wulf
Wulf's Bane
The Last Spook

BROTHER WULF
WULF'S WAR

JOSEPH DELANEY

PUFFIN

N
W
E
S
VALKARKY
CUMULAR MOUNTAINS
PLAINS OF
ERESTABA
GHANBALA
TREE
RIVER SHANNAH
EVERGREEN
PINE FOREST

PUFFIN BOOKS

UK | USA | Canada | Ireland | Australia
India | New Zealand | South Africa

Puffin Books is part of the Penguin Random House group of companies
whose addresses can be found at global.penguinrandomhouse.com.

www.penguin.co.uk
www.puffin.co.uk
www.ladybird.co.uk

First published 2023

001

Text copyright © Joseph Delaney, 2023
Map illustration by Alessia Trunfio

The moral right of the author and illustrator has been asserted

Set in 10/16.5 pt Palatino LT Std
Typeset by Jouve (UK), Milton Keynes
Printed and bound in Great Britain by Clays Ltd, Elcograf S.p.A.

The authorized representative in the EEA is Penguin Random House Ireland,
Morrison Chambers, 32 Nassau Street, Dublin D02 YH68

A CIP catalogue record for this book is available from the British Library

ISBN: 978–0–241–56847–7

All correspondence to:
Puffin Books
Penguin Random House Children's
One Embassy Gardens, 8 Viaduct Gardens, London SW11 7BW

Joseph Delaney
25 July 1945 – 16 August 2022

For Marie
Together again

Penguin Random House Children's are so proud
to have worked with Joseph Delaney for twenty
years to bring his unique blend of fantasy horror
to readers around the world.

Joseph finished writing this book in July 2022,
just four weeks before he died.

What you are about to read is therefore the final,
brilliant outing of the County Spook.

Just remember: it probably shouldn't be read after dark . . .

PROLOGUE

It was dark, and servants of Hell were gathering in the valley ahead: a horde of demons and witches that had travelled from miles around to congregate. Their leader was a monstrous demon with three eyes.

I walked on into the darkness for a while, then I summoned my wolves: Tooth, Claw, Blood, Bone, Hide and Hair. They weren't 'real'. Each was a gristle – and therefore only a magical creation. But they were real enough to help tear our enemies apart.

My name is Wulf. For a time I had trained as a spook's apprentice.

But now I was a tulpar, one with the magical skill to create such beasts.

The wolves bounded towards me out of the darkness.

'There, boys. Calm down now.' I fell to my knees and patted each of them in turn. They were really hungry. Good.

I walked on and they took up their usual positions, three on my right and three on my left. The saliva from their open jaws glistened in the moonlight as it dripped onto the grass.

We'd almost reached the top of the valley now and my heart was starting to beat faster with anticipation and excitement.

There was a faint sound then, carried upon the breeze. It brought the wolves to a sudden halt, their ears flattening backwards. I heard it too. We were listening to distant music.

Pan was playing his pipes.

Some warriors went into battle with the sound of drums to encourage them. I had the pipes of Pan to rouse me to action.

I was the Chipenden Spook, dealing with the dangers from the dark that beset the County – ghosts, ghasts, boggarts and witches. Now I was about to fight a larger battle against forces that had gathered here in vast numbers. They wanted to destroy me.

Because I was no ordinary spook. I was doing more than just keeping local ghouls at bay.

I was fighting a war.

Once, I'd sworn I would serve no god, but in truth I was fighting now on behalf of one of the Old Gods – Pan.

Pan had decided to exterminate the worst demons of the dark, and I was being used as his instrument. He could not fight them directly or he would be destroyed. Years earlier, he had fought the god called Golgoth, the Lord of Winter, and had barely survived, taking years to fully regain his strength. He would not risk that again – and so avoided open conflict against those that opposed him. Thus, a proxy war was being fought against entities who served their masters. They cared nothing for their own survival – they were driven only by a desperate need to destroy me.

Well, good luck to them.

'Seeds!' I cried.

Suddenly my mouth filled with bitter seeds and I spat them onto the ground directly in front of me. This very useful gift had come from Pan. When I called for the seeds, they would come to me and I could use them to create a defensive wall round whatever I wanted.

Within moments of the seeds hitting the ground, thorny vines erupted from the earth and began to race left and right like green fire to encircle the valley. They would soon form an impenetrable barrier with only one entrance, which was directly ahead of me.

'Sword!' I commanded, and there was a pleasing rasp as I heard it insert itself into the empty scabbard upon my back. There was a louder rasp as I reached over my left shoulder and drew it, gripping it firmly with both hands.

Then I gave a third command: 'Thorne!'

Immediately, a silver orb floated down towards me out of the darkness, moving and melding in shape quickly to become a grinning black-skirted girl bristling with blades. Thorne was a witch assassin – a dead one – and the companion of my old witch ally Grimalkin. She had come from the dark at my summons to help me fight our enemies.

The mass of creatures below in the valley was formidable but *I* had chosen the time and place of our encounter. After taking up residence in the Chipenden house, I had shown myself in the village as the new spook.

That had been enough to draw the beasts here.

Now I had to deal with them.

The creatures ran at us, screaming their war cries, voices full of hatred. Many were demons but there were also witches. Some were local but by their distinctive weapons – razors and sharp-toothed blades lashed to long poles – I could see that many had come from Essex, a county far to the south. Years ago, Tom Ward had told me much about these Essex witches. They had always supported the worst elements of the dark and had fought on the side of the Fiend at the Battle of the Wardstone.

But all witches were dangerous. Far stronger than the average man, they could fight with unbridled ferocity. With their fangs and talons they could rip your face to shreds or tear out your throat.

4

Then, among the chaos, I spotted something worse than them – the creature who looked like the leader of this attack: a huge green-scaled demon with three eyes, the largest of which was right at the centre of its forehead. I wanted it destroyed.

I glanced sideways at Thorne and she grinned at me again. She was anything but scared and was clearly looking forward to the fight.

So we ran towards it.

I met the first attack with my sword as I heard Thorne's war cry. Within seconds, three lay dead at my feet. I had shifted my body to my warrior tulpa form, and it displayed its usual precision of movement in combat. Thorne was also using her blades deftly, pressing forward skilfully. She had been trained by Grimalkin and, as such, was a formidable fighter. The grey wolves were savaging any enemy in sight. The battle was going well.

My aim was to ensure that no servant of the dark left the valley alive. I glanced around, searching for the green triple-eyed demon. I knew that it was powerful and had been a close supporter of the Fiend – I had once been told by a friend that it was one of the Devil's sons.

Occasionally, I caught a glimpse of it, fangs bared in a snarl as it urged its minions forward. If the fight went our way, eventually it would be the only one left standing. Then it would be forced to confront us directly and I would deal with it.

At times we were pressed hard and twice there was a real threat that we would be overwhelmed. But we stood firm and began to force our foes back. I had created only one narrow entrance to the circle of thorns that encircled the valley. With Thorne on my right and the wolves – three on our right and three on our left – the creatures had no means of escape. We marched down the incline slaying our enemies with each step forward.

Then it was over at last. I was grateful that none of us had been badly hurt. A couple of the wolves were licking their wounds but we were mostly unscathed.

Now we had to deal with the bodies of our enemies. My wolves were feeding on some of them – it was their right, as they were legitimate kills. Some of the demons they wouldn't touch, but I couldn't simply leave them slain here. If left, dead witches' bodies would be touched by the light of the full moon, upon which they would become undead, able to wander the earth and seek out victims. Some were weak and could only crawl through the trees eating worms, slugs and other small creatures. But occasionally one became strong enough to run and catch any human prey foolish enough to pass close to them after dark.

Suddenly I had a moment of inspiration. Using my mind, I directed the vicious thorn vines to wrap themselves round each dead demon or witch, and drag them down into the earth. Each would have an unmarked grave. That way their fellow witches could not locate them here and potentially try to revive them.

But there were too many of them.

Thorne helped me drag the rest of the dead witches back to the Chipenden house where I immediately spent the rest of the night and the first part of the morning digging three deep new pits.

I was exhausted but I still wasn't done . . . I went down into the village and hired the local blacksmith and stonemason to do the rest of the necessary work. They were used to a spook's requests and no questions were asked. Instead they quickly constructed bars over the pits, and entombed the pit in stone. That should keep the dead witches confined – just in case.

At last, the job was done: the witches were tipped into the pits and the bars were set in position. With the County safe once again, I was exhausted and, after a thorough wash, went to bed.

But it was only moments before my eyes closed that I remembered something. Something very important.

My utter weariness had fogged my memory until now.

One of the demons was unaccounted for.

The huge green-scaled demon with three eyes – the leader of the horde. Where was it?

I hadn't seen it as the battle had ended. How had it escaped? Now that I thought about it, I realized that the harder I had fought to reach the three-eyed demon, the greater the distance had become that divided us. Powerful dark magic had clearly been worked against me.

I was uneasy. The night had not been quite as successful as I'd planned. But I was also exhausted and, for now, my failure did not prevent me from quickly dropping off to sleep.

In the morning I would recommence my duties as the Chipenden Spook.

THE FIRST WARNING

I gazed at the garden in astonishment. Although it was early June, the leaves were already falling.

That was my first warning that something was badly wrong – my first intimation that I was in deadly danger. We had won the great battle, but the war against the dark had entered a critical stage, and my partnership with Pan suddenly seemed worrying. He was the God of Nature. So why were the leaves falling so early? How could he let this happen?

Something must be badly wrong, and I needed his strength in the war against the dark. If all was not well then we could be in real danger.

I strode away from the Chipenden house and looked up at the trees again. The leaves that were still attached to the branches looked tired and discoloured, and were starting to shrivel.

I looked down too at the dead leaves scattered across the grass. I'd first noticed them the previous day but there had been fewer and I'd been off on spook's business – an urgent call to deal with a particularly destructive boggart – so I hadn't really taken much notice. But I was taking notice now and I didn't like what I saw.

Who could change the seasons, changing what Pan ordained for our world? The first name that came to my mind was Golgoth. Was that Old God fighting Pan again and now exerting his icy strength to bring winter to the County before it was due? Or did this threat extend beyond the County? It was something that I urgently needed to find out.

Although I was not the seventh son of a seventh son, I had become the Chipenden Spook without hesitation. I was fitted for the role because of my powers as a tulpar, meaning I had the ability to make the creatures that I conjured within my imagination take real physical form in the world. Some of these tulpas, called wraiths, I could inhabit – each was a body that I could pull on or temporarily cast off like a coat.

I did that now, exchanging my human form for that of the sky wolf. Seconds later I was soaring aloft, each beat of my powerful black wings carrying me higher. I kept my size relatively small – no larger than a kestrel hawk – and achieved sufficient altitude so that I wouldn't attract attention from watchers on the ground. By keeping myself small I conserved energy; it was strength I might require if located and attacked while I was flying and then needed to increase my size to be more effective in combat.

I crossed Chipenden village and then flew east, following the River Ribble towards Pendle.

My eyes were not human and were suited to flight so I could see the different swathes of colour intertwining in the air. Some were brown thermals, air heated by the sun, that I could use to rise higher, thus further conserving my own strength. I could also see small creatures moving in the hedgerows that if I were hungry could become my prey. But as I flew eastwards, I was more interested in the ground – I studied the woods far below me, examining their canopies of leaves.

The change in colour was slight. After all, the process had probably only been underway for a couple of days. But it was there all right, as far as my keen eyes could see. Autumn had arrived in June.

I was heading for the border between the County and Yorkshire and soon it came into view, the River Calder reflecting the sunlight. I soared across it and immediately noticed the difference in the weather below. I flew north then and checked the border with Cumbria, the peaks of the Lake District shining in the sunlight. It was the same – a sudden transition from June weather to the onset of autumn chills. I flew south and west – Morecambe Bay and the Irish

Sea sparkling in the sunlight – until the border with Cymru was below me.

It was exactly the same. Winter was coming early to the County but everywhere else was untouched.

There were demons and witches everywhere, but spooks from the County *had* done more damage to the dark than anywhere else. Generations of spooks had fought to keep it at bay. My old master, Tom Ward, had been responsible for the death of Siscoi, the Vampire God, and had also slain the Fiend. Witches, despite their stronghold in Pendle, had largely been confined there and kept in check. Thus, the County was the place the dark would probably most like to hurt.

And there was my recent slaying of the servants of the dark in our battle in the valley near Chipenden. Was this now being done in revenge?

Was I the main target? Pan *must* be in danger – or at least his power had clearly been limited in some way. I needed to find out what was happening, and I knew there was one person who might well be able to supply the answer.

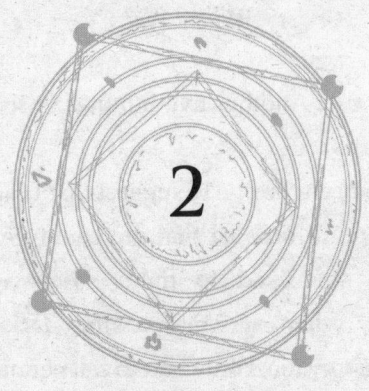

THORNE

Grimalkin, the witch assassin, had been an ally of my old friends Alice and Tom during their many years' fighting the dark. Grimalkin was dead, slain by Golgoth. Her flesh and bones had been frozen and shattered into pieces but she still survived dwelling within the dark and had been steadily growing more powerful. She could visit the earth, but only during the hours of darkness because the light of the sun would destroy her.

I needed her now but did not know how to contact her.

But, of course, I did know how to contact Thorne – still Grimalkin's companion in the dark. She was able to come to my side if I simply called her name, as she had done so in battle. That was enough to summon her after dark.

So now I was sitting at the withy trees crossroads beneath the bell that was customarily rung to call the Spook from the

Chipenden house. Another five minutes or so and it would be dark enough.

Thorne had been the one to suggest that I call her down to earth from time to time so that we could be companions. Especially as she liked to fight. So as we'd recently demonstrated, when servants of the dark gathered in numbers to destroy me, I only had to call her name and she'd battle alongside me.

I had shifted my shape again and wasn't in the shape of the warrior, that form which I presented to the world when I was on spook's business. Now, I inhabited the tulpa of the boy Wulf, the one who had become a novice monk, then later a spook's apprentice and finally the trainee of a dead tulpar called Hrothgar.

I had chosen to be the boy Wulf because that was the form I had been in when I first met Thorne and I knew that she liked it best. Actually I worried that she liked me in ways I did not reciprocate.

In the distance an owl called out into the darkness, while bats began to flitter overhead, gliding between the willow trees. It was time.

'Thorne!' I called out into the darkness.

She responded almost immediately. A silver sphere descended towards me, swooped below the branches, settled on the grass and immediately took on the form of the young female witch assassin, her blades as usual mainly worn in sheaths in diagonal leather straps across the front of her body. Her skirt was split and tied to her legs to afford her ease of mobility when fighting. I knew she would have weapons concealed elsewhere as Grimalkin would have taught her. She also had a necklace of thumb-bones around her neck. They had been taken from defeated enemies and each one was filled with magical power which she could draw upon at will.

Usually, she grinned at me in anticipation that I had summoned her to earth, but I was surprised to see that today the expression on her face – much like my own – was one of sadness with a hint of fear.

'I thought you'd never send for me or were unable to do so. I feared you might already be dead!' she exclaimed.

I patted the grass and she sat down opposite me. 'What made you think that?' I asked. 'And if you thought so then why didn't you visit me?'

'I couldn't. Three nights ago, Grimalkin left the dark to visit the County. She didn't tell me why and she went alone. But she never came back. If she was unable to take refuge from the sunlight, by now she'll have been destroyed. The following night I intended to follow and search for her, but found I couldn't. The cauldron at the crossroads has been destroyed or hidden from me. Without it I cannot visit the earth. I just hoped that you would still be alive and have the power to call me here.'

I pondered this. Grimalkin and Thorne had slain the goddess Hecate and taken possession of her cauldron, which enabled them to visit any place on earth after dark. They had killed her by pushing her into her own pot – and later they had done the same to the terrible goddess Circe, after I had fought and weakened her. Who would know to destroy this cauldron?

'What about Pan?' I asked her. 'Something must be wrong for the leaves to fall in the County so early. Do you know anything of that?'

Thorne shook her head. 'You know Pan dwells on his own island in the dark and certainly doesn't welcome visitors. But if you hadn't summoned me tonight, I had intended to visit him to ask for his help in locating Grimalkin and the cauldron – even if it meant risking his anger.'

This would have been a very dangerous action to take. Pan didn't welcome people to his lair, and to go there uninvited was to risk his terrible wrath.

I nodded. 'Where did Grimalkin disappear? In which part of the County?'

'A place called Silverdale, far in the north of the County.'

'Quite some distance,' I said. 'It's near the border with Cumbria. Did she tell you why she was going there?'

Thorne shook her head. 'She didn't tell me everything. But most of her secrets were to protect me. I suspect she thought she was going to be in danger and didn't want me to face the same peril.'

'I'll set off at dawn tomorrow,' I told Thorne. 'It'll take me most of the daylight hours to get there. As soon as it's dark I'll call you to me and we can search for Grimalkin.'

'Why don't you become the sky wolf and fly there now?'

'I've already spent several hours as a sky wolf today; spending so long in the same shape carries a risk of forgetting what it's like to be human.'

She nodded. 'Yes. You do know that it could be a trap to lure you there by those who know of your and Grimalkin's allegiance? Have you considered that?'

'That's possible. But I intend to be very cautious.' I felt calm about what faced me. 'And you'll be with me, I hope.'

'Nothing would please me more, Wulf, than to be by your side tomorrow. That's what I hoped you'd say.'

'Have you sensed that *you* were in danger recently? Have you noticed any changes to the dark?'

Thorne shrugged. 'I know that we're being watched more closely than usual. Grimalkin warned me to take special care. Different factions are contending to produce a new ruler of the dark and they're seeking out potential enemies or allies. But that's nothing new, simply the routine cycle that always occurs.'

I came to my feet and she did the same and faced me. Then she reached across, gripped my hand and squeezed it, smiling into my eyes, reminding me of my worry that she wanted to be more than just a friend and warrior companion.

I liked Thorne a lot. But the truth was I could not get the thought of Tilda, the daughter of Tom Ward and Alice, from my mind.

My last visit to the dark had proved costly. I had fought and defeated the Fiend soon after he had regenerated and returned to power. But I had been poisoned during our fight, cut by his deadly fangs and talons. Only the intervention of Pan had saved me from death. But something else had happened to change the direction of my life. The living are not meant to dwell in the dark. If they stay for too long, time passes much faster on earth, and so it was for me. I arrived back in Chipenden almost a century later to find Alice, Tom and Tilda dead – presumably of old age. Their graves were in the garden close to where John Gregory, the Spook, had been buried years earlier. I had been deeply upset.

There had been no grave for Jenny, the girl who had been Tom's apprentice at the time. I had no idea what had happened to her, but assumed that, as a hundred years or so had passed on earth, surely she was also dead.

Although I knew it was far longer in reality, for me less than a year had gone by since I had last seen Tilda. Even though I knew she was dead, I could not push aside her memory so easily and give my love to Thorne. But now I did not push Thorne away either. I let her continue to hold my hand while gazing into her eyes and smiling. She was my friend and I didn't want to hurt her feelings.

At last, she released my hand and stepped back. 'Until tomorrow night, Wulf!' Then she gave me a wave before transforming again into a silver sphere and soaring above the willow trees to become a faint star which eventually winked out in the blackness of the sky.

I walked back into the garden, climbing upwards towards the house. Tomorrow night we would search for Grimalkin. I hoped that she had survived whatever had happened to her, but I was not optimistic. I knew the rules that limited her survival on earth and now I knew that she had been here three days – that was certainly not something that she would have done by choice.

The war was rumbling on. And it felt like we were on the back foot.

THE WRITING ON THE WALL

Soon after dawn, I walked down through the garden. The scattering of leaves on the grass had become a carpet and the tree canopy above my head was thinning rapidly.

There was a chill wind blowing from the east, hastening the change of season, and I was glad of my spook's cloak with its warm hood that I wore over my chain-mail armour. I was back in the warrior tulpa form I usually took when on spook's business – but I had made another change to the traditions of the County Spook. In addition to a great fighting staff, I carried an empty scabbard on my back. One word from me and it would fill with the special sword that had been loaned to me – only to come when I most needed it – by the Piper, an acquaintance of Grimalkin and one of the few allies that I had in the dark.

On earth the Piper had been a powerful mage and still retained much of that power in the dark. Using his pipes, he controlled an army of intelligent but ferocious rats and I suspected that he had other powers that I had not yet seen.

Setting off now, I was glad it was June and the days were at their longest. If I walked fast, I estimated that I would arrive at my destination an hour or so before dusk, which would be just time enough to rest and gather my strength for whatever danger I faced. I'd eaten little of my breakfast, earning a growl of annoyance from Kratch, the boggart who guarded the Chipenden house and garden and did the cooking – but I'd brought with me a small amount of the best County crumbly cheese to eat on the journey. This was a tradition that I *did* follow; spooks over many generations had fuelled themselves this way.

I climbed Parlick Pike, then headed north, reaching Caster early in the afternoon. Normally a spook would skirt round this city, as often a quisitor would be based in the castle. Despite our work protecting the County, quisitors considered spooks no better than witches and to fall into their hands would mean a short trial, torture and then a burning at the stake.

But this was not a normal situation, and I was no ordinary spook, and I had no time for detours. So I crossed the cobbled streets of the city in the form of Piddle, a small dog tulpa, who attracted glances of dislike and a readiness of every passing stranger to kick out at him. Piddle's tail was more suited to that of a rat, and his coat was mangy.

His senses were different from human ones. In particular his ability to detect and discriminate between odours was very powerful, and in occupying his form I could often smell the tell-tale stink of humans that told me much about them and what they had been up to recently.

Once within the city I joined the course of the canal and followed its left bank northwards. Only when far beyond Caster did I take the form of the warrior again. After a while I passed the bell that was positioned so that callers could summon a spook from the old millhouse. It had been occupied for many years by Bill Arkwright and then by Judd Brinscall, and finally by Spook Johnson – another old master of mine. All three men were long dead now. The first two had been killed by the servants of the dark and I had no idea what fate had befallen Johnson. Eventually, I knew I would have to spend some time at the millhouse. Water witches would be gathering on the marsh in larger and larger numbers. But, for now, there were far more important things to deal with.

So I continued north along the towpath. Occasionally I passed narrowboats with their many different cargoes. Some, brightly painted and well maintained, carried textiles or food and others were coal barges covered in soot and grime. My staff, distinctive cloak and hood clearly indicated that I was a spook. I attracted plenty of friendly waves, which was unusual because folk were often nervous being in the vicinity of a spook, thinking that he was never very far away from some creature of the dark.

Maybe these people thought that a spook was returning to the area and welcomed that possibility, hoping for a reduction in the dangers they faced every day.

I realized that some of the water witches on the marsh might have transferred themselves to the canal. A bargeman would have little protection against the taloned hand of a witch that might reach up from below to grab his ankle and drag him down into the water. He would be drained of blood quickly, long before he had time to drown. When I'd been apprenticed to Spook Johnson I had fought them myself. I knew just how deadly and dangerous they could be.

Eventually, I left the canal bank, taking the path that led to the northwest. It would take me closer to Morecambe Bay and to my final destination which was the village of Silverdale. I'd never visited there but I had heard much good about it from Tom Ward and Spook Johnson, both of whom really liked the place. In addition to the scenic views, its people were friendly and generous with their hospitality.

What had brought Grimalkin to Silverdale and what had happened to her there?

*

Gazing down upon the waters of the estuary, the bay beyond sparkling in the sunlight, Silverdale certainly lived up to its picturesque reputation.

It was late but I could still see people going about their business. Despite their reputation for friendliness, it was better not to make my presence known. I sat with my back to a wall and nibbled a little crumbly cheese as I waited for dusk. Once it arrived, I took another precaution, exchanging the tulpa of the warrior for that of Piddle again.

Not only would the little dog attract relatively little attention, I needed his sensitive nose. If Grimalkin was down there in Silverdale, he would soon sniff her out.

It was dark when I found the first trace of the witch assassin.

No sooner had I located her distinctive scent than I changed into the tulpa of Wulf, complete with staff and bag. I called out, 'Thorne!' and the silver sphere floated down out of the darkness. I smiled a welcome at her as she appeared at my side.

'She *was* inside there,' I told Thorne, pointing at the large coach house in front of us. 'I don't think she still is but it's worth taking a look anyway.'

The inn next to it was closed and in darkness, but I thought I could hear horses snorting and stirring in the coach house.

I changed my form again into Saint Quentin, the patron saint of locksmiths. I reached out my bony arm, gripping a key in my gnarled hand, taking but seconds to deal with the simple lock. I quickly changed once more – this time into the form of the warrior again, more suited to combat if danger were to threaten – and I led the way inside.

There were indeed horses in the stalls at the far end of the building, and they snorted uneasily at our presence. More impressive than them though was the large vehicle directly before us. The coach was huge, well constructed from ornate, black-painted wood – and unusually it had two doors but no windows.

'They could have used this to transport Grimalkin,' Thorne said. 'It would have kept her safe from the sunlight.'

I nodded, trying to maintain hope that the witch assassin hadn't been destroyed. Changing back into Piddle, a quick sniff confirmed this. 'We need to find out where they've taken her,' I told Thorne after I'd changed into the warrior again.

Outside once more in the form of Piddle, with Thorne flying alongside me in the form of the silver sphere, I soon picked up the trail. They had carried her north towards the County border with Cumbria. To hasten things along as we travelled, I frequently changed form into the sky wolf. But those periods of flight I kept to a minimum and I spent a lot of time walking.

There were good reasons that I didn't spend longer than necessary in the shape of the sky wolf. One danger for a tulpar was creating too many bodies to inhabit. If he did that, his soul could be dissipated and he could weaken and decline until he ceased to be. The other threat was spending too long in the same shape. You could end up as a permanent sky wolf and forget everything you had ever been and done. So, because of those threats, I had become more cautious and economical about shifting my shape.

There could have been no other way the coach had travelled than this narrow road that led northwards but, every so often, I used Piddle's senses to check the surface just in case. We were probably dealing with powerful dark magic here – how else would they have overcome the formidable Grimalkin? – so we had to be alert for deceptions that might take us away from where she might really have been taken. Powerful spells could hide paths or conceal a coach.

Grimalkin had once seemed undefeatable and only growing in power. With Thorne's help she'd destroyed two goddesses of the dark and Thorne had adopted a boastful title to crown themselves with: *Slayers of Gods*! But now they had lost control of the cauldron and the freedom to visit the earth at will. Not only that, in the dark, I had recently had to save Grimalkin from certain destruction at the hands of the Fiend's servants. It was a hard thing to accept but Grimalkin was no longer the powerful force that she'd once been. Either that or the forces that opposed her were rapidly growing in power and becoming unassailable.

I didn't know what was going on. But all I could do right now was follow her scent.

As it was June, the hours of darkness were short. But by the time Thorne was forced to leave my side, I'd identified where the coach had headed.

As a spook's apprentice, it had been part of my training to study the layout of the County and the lands that bordered it. I had memorized many maps and, soon after passing close to the shore of Lake Windermere, still heading north, it became clear that the windowless coach had been taking Grimalkin towards a town called Keswick. Whether it was where she was now held, only time would tell, but I said farewell to Thorne, who reluctantly returned to the dark only after we'd agreed to meet again at dusk, and after nibbling a little more cheese, I climbed over a drystone wall and grabbed a couple of hours' sleep.

Waking, I immediately continued north towards Keswick, walking fast.

The clouds were low and dark grey, obscuring the tops of the fells which seemed to close in on either side threateningly as if advancing towards me. Soon I'd left Windermere far behind and was walking along the eastern shore of another smaller lake.

By now, I was hungry. In the form of the sky wolf I would have been looking forward to the taste of hot warm flesh and blood but as the boy Wulf I noticed a large inn ahead – and at the thought of a warm steak and ale pie my stomach started growling.

The inn was positioned on the right-hand side of the lake opposite the shore. I strolled inside, approached the counter and ordered a large slice of pie with potatoes and peas. There were a couple of farm labourers leaning on the counter supping mugs of ale. They gave me wary glances so I simply nodded towards them then left them alone, spotting a small snug, a side room, where I would be free from curious eyes who might wonder about the visit of a spook.

I leaned my staff against the wall, sat down and glanced across towards the narrow wood-panelled room's only other occupants: a mother and child.

The pie was delicious and I made short work of it. I was just forking up the last of my peas when I glanced across towards the far end of the room. The child, who looked to be a girl of about seven or eight, was facing her mother across the table, her hands resting on its edge and leaning forward to be fed. The mother, a robust red-faced woman, was feeding her from a spoon which she kept dipping into a thick meaty gravy before easing it into the child's eager mouth.

For a second, I thought nothing of it but then the child dropped onto all fours and turned her head to look back towards me.

My blood ran cold. It was not a child. It was a pug-faced short-haired dog, garbed in a long dress. What I had taken for shoes was black fur.

I glanced away and calmed myself down. It was strange to dress a dog in the clothes of a human and then feed it from your own spoon. But it was none of my business.

I set about minding my own affairs once again but when the woman and dog passed by me to leave the snug, I could clearly see that it was not a dog. It was a human child again!

Or at least it had the appearance of a child. No doubt most people would not have seen the truth of the matter, but I had some immunity against witches and was not always deceived by their spells. I'd been sharing the small room with a witch and her familiar. She'd been using a spell of illusion to conceal the familiar, something similar to a 'glamour', which was used by a witch to make herself more attractive to men.

As a spook, it was my duty to deal with her. But I'd more pressing concerns right now. Maybe once I'd found Grimalkin I could revisit this area and hunt this witch down. After paying for my meal and going back outside, neither the witch nor the familiar were anywhere to be seen. Just in case, I briefly became Piddle again and tried to sniff out and remember their acrid scent. But they seemed to have moved on.

Then I continued north, walking steadily until soon after dusk when once again I spoke 'Thorne!' and a silver sphere floated down out of the mist before taking the assassin's form and walking beside me.

It soon became clear to us that Grimalkin was not being held within Keswick itself. As we approached the town, Piddle's senses quickly picked up that the captive witch assassin's present location was southeast of the town – somewhere elevated, it seemed.

We found a small cottage by the side of the road, almost directly opposite a narrow path that looked like it would take us up a hill to where we wanted to be.

An old man was heading towards his front door, and as we approached him he turned, a startled expression on his lined face, before taking a quick terrified step backwards. Not that I could blame him – I must have seemed threatening enough but Thorne, with her bristling blades and teeth filed to points, looked demonic.

'We mean you no harm,' I said, in a wasted attempt to reassure him. 'We only want to know what's up there?' I pointed back towards the path behind us.

He opened his mouth and tried to speak but it was his third mumbled attempt before I could make out what he was saying.

'Castlerigg Stones!' he blurted. 'An evil place. Haunted, it is. Folks keep well away!' He wagged his finger towards us. 'Never step inside that circle!'

Then he opened his door and scuttled inside, slamming it hard behind him. I could hear him clanging home the bolts to secure himself as best he could for the night.

'Well, a reaction like that means we must be in the right place!' Thorne had a dark smile on her face.

'Indeed,' I agreed. I wondered what we were about to face.

We turned our backs on the cottage. And, in case our approach was watched, without discussing it we decided to climb to the southeast, the edge of the town gradually falling away behind us. Our destination wasn't a dwelling from what the scents I'd picked up could tell – at least, not one inhabited by humans. I wondered if it might be standing stones. They were ancient and often haunted by malevolent spirits, or simply attractive to dangerous entities from the dark.

It was a relatively steep ascent and we breathed heavily. We were climbing above the low cloud and mist, and soon the moon and stars were visible and the drizzle eased away to almost nothing.

It was indeed stones at the top: a large circle of ancient stones gleaming in the moonlight. I'd expected something less significant – having never heard of this place before – and its size took me by surprise: it must have been about one hundred feet in diameter and was made up of more than forty standing stones of varying sizes. When I'd studied maps as Spook Johnson's apprentice, I'd committed many routes, towns and villages to memory and had seen quite a few stone circles when travelling to hunt witches, but this was by far the largest and most impressive.

Thorne and I walked away from the circle to get a view of it set against the background of encircling fells and mountains from a distance. When we came up against the drystone wall boundary of the large field, I glanced down in the direction of Keswick. There was nothing to be seen but grey mist so we walked slowly back towards the circle. There were sheep grazing in the field and we needed to be careful where we stepped.

Then Thorne noticed something. 'Look what a lovely present one of the sheep has left us!' She laughed at first, pointing at the grass. 'It's left us a diagram of the positions of the stones!'

I glanced down and saw to my astonishment that she was perfectly correct. The dark blobs of excrement formed a pattern of stones that seemed almost identical to the actual stone circle. This was true of the relative size and position of each deposit.

I shivered. Some strange intelligence or dark magic was at work here. This was a step too far to be mere coincidence. No ordinary sheep could have done this.

When comparing the stones to the pattern on the grass I noticed something unusual that most stone circles did not have. There were thirteen extra stones *within* the circle, back against its edge. Some were flat and low and suggestive of foundations of a building.

I made to step inside them. But Thorne reached for my arm, affected by the change in atmosphere: 'What about the old man's warning?'

I knew we had to step inside despite the risks. 'We must just be careful, Thorne. Keep our wits about us.' I stepped firmly forward.

But even as Thorne nodded grimly, gripping her blades in response as she followed me into the circle, the air shimmered. I looked up to see that the stars had disappeared and the sky was now a baleful red. There was a strange shape in the distance.

We had entered an underworld.

'It's no wonder the locals stay away,' I told Thorne. 'Imagine blundering into this ill-prepared!'

'Strange that it's not protected,' said Thorne.

That was true. Underworlds were often the lairs of creatures that preyed upon humans, and were sometimes also bridges to the dark itself. But although their creators liked to enter and leave them at will, a magical barrier often prevented unwary humans from wandering inside. That had been the case with the underworld that had been created and owned by Hrothgar. But this one seemed to have no such defences.

The shape in the distance had been visible from the moment we'd entered the magical zone, the very second that the sky had become red, but at Thorne's gasp I realized that we hadn't recognized it for what it truly was. At first glance it had seemed no more than some natural large edifice of rocks, jutting up from the ground.

Now we could see that there were doors and windows. They were unusual in their various shapes – distorted geometry rather than the usual regular squares and oblongs that were the portals of most human dwellings. The windows were translucent but did not offer a clear view into the interior of the strange house. In fact, they appeared to be made of crystal rather than glass. And the one door visible was constructed from an odd triangular-shaped slab of heavy stone. I certainly wouldn't be using my boot to break that open!

I changed back into the Piddle tulpa and ran forward across the grass to halt before it. One quick sniff told me that Grimalkin was somewhere inside. We had reached her!

Back in the shape of the warrior I turned towards Thorne who could tell the good news from my face.

'She's here?!' she asked excitedly.

'Yes, but the problem's going to be getting inside,' I told her while we gazed at that formidable door.

There was writing engraved into the stone above it:

Non Generant Aquilae Columbash!

I had been a noviciate monk and had studied Latin. This was easy to translate: *Eagles Do Not Breed Doves!*

As I was digesting this, to my astonishment the stone door began to open, grinding and grating as it eased slowly back, swivelling on invisible hinges. Moments later it gaped wide. We could see nothing within – only a yawning darkness, a black mouth waiting to swallow us. The door might close again at any moment, so I quickly stepped inside, gesturing Thorne to follow.

Immediately, candles – dozens of them – ignited, filling a small anteroom with flickering yellow light. The claustrophobic room was more like a cave, replete with stone shelves upon which the wax candles were clustered and bonded to the rock with coils and globules of dripped wax. There was an inner door, perfectly oblong, about six feet high and constructed of stout polished oak but with no visible handle or lock.

Would this door open too to welcome us within? Who was in control here?

There was no sign of immediate danger, so I spent a few seconds in the form of Piddle, alert to every scent and sound. The strange house was in silence, but I sensed that there was someone waiting in the inner room – more than one entity. I thought that they must be fully aware that we were standing just outside the door. They had opened the stone door to admit us – why not do the same with this wooden one?

Thorne pointed silently down to the floor with a questioning look.

I agreed that Grimalkin was probably somewhere underground – maybe imprisoned in some sort of cellar.

Thorne and I looked at each other. We knew without a word that we had few options here but to attack. Ease of entry to such a place surely meant it was a trap.

I quickly changed into the warrior tulpa.

'Sword!' I commanded, and there was a loud rasp as the sword given to me by the Piper slid into the scabbard on my back. I drew it, gripping it firmly with both hands.

'Better knock and let them know we're coming in!' grinned Thorne, drawing two blades of her own with a flourish. 'After all, it's only polite!'

I smiled but my knock was far from polite – a forceful blow from my heavy right boot that smashed the door inwards, splintering the edges of the wood and hurling it back against the inner wall with a loud thud.

I stepped into the room, weapon readied to do what was necessary. The warrior tulpa was very economical in combat. Each blow could be a killing stroke. I would slay our enemies quickly and then we would go down into the cellar and rescue Grimalkin.

But it was not necessary to attack.

Stunned, I stared in astonishment at the two people who faced me.

It was Tom Ward and Alice Deane.

4

DECEPTIONS

Tom and Alice appeared as though well into their sixties, with grey hair and lined faces. Tom looked relatively frail – far from the spook who would run miles when an emergency demanded it – but Alice still seemed full of vitality; they were exactly as I remembered them when we had last met over a century earlier.

How could they be here after so many years had passed? And what about their graves at Chipenden? And then, of course, Tilda came to my thoughts. What had happened to her? Was she still alive also? My hopes soared.

The room was quite small and was unfurnished. It had a flagged floor and there were stone steps on the right, no doubt leading down to a cellar. Tom Ward's staff rested against the wall in the far corner of the room and I noticed too late that he was gripping a silver chain.

Before I could react, he used it.

Tom cast the chain with his left hand, sending it towards the ceiling before it fell in a spiral towards its intended target.

His aim was as good as ever. It was a perfect cast and it fell onto Thorne, binding her arms to her sides and her legs together. It also achieved what spooks called *spread*, the chain tight across her mouth and right down to almost her ankles.

Unable to cry out or utter spells, Thorne fell to her knees, the blades falling from her hands to clatter upon the flags, her eyes burning into mine.

For a moment the only sound was a rasp as I re-drew my sword.

'Put it away!' Alice cried. 'It had to be done, Wulf, as soon you'll realize. Ain't good things we have to tell you, but they're the plain and honest truth. Tom just saved us all!'

I kept the sword in a two-handed grip as I briefly met Thorne's eyes. A great deal was whirling through my head.

'The new threat from the dark is from Grimalkin and her companion here: Thorne.' Tom gestured towards my friend. 'They've kept their plans well hidden for a long time but their intentions are to rule the dark and what they've got planned for folk on earth is as bad as what the Fiend once intended. You will have noticed the weather changing?' He paused and looked at me intently.

I nodded and so he continued. 'After Golgoth freezes the County so that thousands die of cold and famine, dark entities obedient to Grimalkin will walk the earth and make it their own . . .'

'But there's a chance to stop that. We have Grimalkin bound and safe below us,' Alice said, pointing to the steps leading downwards. 'All that remained was to lure Thorne here. So, we're really sorry for the deceptions, Wulf, but we'd no choice but to deceive you, had we? All for the best, ain't it?'

I glanced down at Thorne who was trembling from head to foot. And although I didn't like to see her in pain, there was something I disliked even more. If her suffering was true then this deception was larger than even Alice admitted.

A witch could be bound with a silver-alloy chain and made helpless. But Thorne was a *dead* witch who usually dwelt in the dark. The chain should not have had such a devastating effect as it now seemed to be having. Both Grimalkin and Thorne were strong assassins who, even when still alive, had trained themselves to resist the hurtful effects of silver. So this should not be happening.

Then there were the graves at the Chipenden house. If this was Tom and Alice, then who was buried there?

'I've seen your graves,' I told them.

'Ain't so, Wulf,' Alice protested. 'Those graves are empty. That was necessary to keep our enemies at bay. We've survived through a hundred years or more of earth time by living within this underworld. You know how that works.'

I certainly did and couldn't deny that was a possibility. To my cost, I'd experienced such different flows of time myself. What she said made a sort of sense but there were too many warnings shrilling inside my head to ignore. I had fought beside Grimalkin and Thorne many times and I could not accept what was being said about them.

'I trust Grimalkin and Thorne,' I told Alice. 'I find it hard to believe your accusations. We've fought battles together more times than I can remember. They recently helped me to destroy the Fiend!'

'Of course they did, Wulf!' Alice exclaimed, shaking her head and smiling as if at my foolishness. 'What else *would* they have done? It was in their own interests to destroy other rulers of the dark. They were clearing the way for their own reign of terror! That's what they've been doing since Grimalkin was slain by Golgoth and entered the dark. And what about the many times that *we've* fought together? Have you forgotten all that?'

I had forgotten nothing. I owed Tom and Alice a large debt. They had both been fearsome fighters of the dark. But although what she said *did* make sense, I was still not convinced.

If I was wrong, what I was about to do would prove harmless.

We'd be able to laugh about it together.

But I didn't think that would happen. Piddle knew the scent of Tom and Alice. But the little dog had not detected it anywhere within this strange house when he'd picked up Grimalkin.

'You are *not* Tom Ward and Alice Deane!' I challenged them. 'You are both tulpas!'

Immediately, Alice staggered and her eyes rolled up into her head. In a moment both creatures were writhing on the flags, beginning to disintegrate.

There came a muffled yelp of what I assumed was triumph from Thorne.

Of course it was not Tom and Alice. These entities were tulpas just as I had suspected, but not the type called wraiths that I inhabited. They were gristles, like my wolves – those who led an independent life from their creator – and whoever that was in this case, they were clearly dark and powerful. Shaped from blood, bone dust, clay and vegetable matter, these two in front of me were now violently reverting to those components, moaning in pain as it happened. Their torment was more mental than physical but it was still difficult to watch and I was forced to turn my face away.

They would have actually *believed* they were who they claimed to be. They'd been telling the truth as far as they understood it. It was a terrible shock for a tulpa to realize what it really was – a thing without a soul, about to enter oblivion.

When I looked at them again, all that remained were a few rags and shallow heaps of slime. The silver chain had fallen into dust, as had the semblance of a spook's staff which had been resting against the wall. Both had been part of the tulpa, just as when I took the shape of the boy Wulf, my own staff was a part of my tulpa.

I helped the now-freed Thorne to her feet. She was still trembling. 'Tulpas!' she said. 'But who could have created them?'

I shook my head. Who indeed? The only tulpar that I'd ever met was Hrothgar and he was gone, having died in the dark long ago, according to earth time.

'Let's not forget why we're in this godforsaken place!' Thorne pulled me back to the present. 'Let us find Grimalkin.'

With her in front, we went down the steps to find that Grimalkin was already free, the fetters that held her also having disintegrated as the tulpas ceased to exist. The cellar was small with an earthen floor but there was a narrow tunnel leading from it.

'You took your time!' The witch assassin was as stern as ever.

But she smiled at me and then she and Thorne hugged. They were like mother and daughter in many respects. Only when they had finished their brief reunion with a whispered conversation did they turn back to speak to me.

'Obviously this underworld must have been constructed by or at least inhabited by another tulpar, Wulf,' Grimalkin told me. 'Find that being and no doubt he'll lead us to the enemy that seeks to control the dark and destroy Pan.'

'It's good to see you, Grimalkin,' I told her. 'But why did you go to Silverdale?' I asked. 'What led you there?'

'Pan has recently come under attack many times by an alliance of gods – his domain is under siege. It was Pan who sent word. He said that an enemy lurked in Silverdale. He was correct, but it was a trap and I was briefly fooled by those tulpas, thinking they really were Tom and Alice. Then it was too late and I fell into their hands. I thought that Thorne would soon come to my aid – when she didn't, I knew that something was badly wrong.'

'I can no longer find the crossroads and the cauldron, Grimalkin,' Thorne said. 'It's been hidden from us. But for Wulf summoning me, I would now be unable to leave the dark.'

'So, the same may be true for me,' Grimalkin wondered out loud. 'But until we can find the crossroads, there may be another way to reach the earth,' she said, pointing towards the narrow tunnel that led from the corner of the earthen cellar. 'Most underworlds join the earth to the dark. If we can find the portal, we can use that to get here whenever we like.'

'I'll come with you,' I said. 'I agree it would be useful to explore the tunnels. I'd like to learn more about the tulpar responsible for this.'

Grimalkin shook her head. 'It's not worth the risk to you, Wulf. Time seems stable here at the moment but there's no guarantee it will continue that way. It is better to enter this underworld infrequently and keep your stays here as short as possible. If things go well, we could meet on the outside of the stone circle after dusk tomorrow.'

Reluctantly I nodded. Grimalkin was right. We needed to be cautious.

Thorne squeezed my hand quickly, smiled, then she walked away with Grimalkin into the darkness of that narrow earthen tunnel. I felt a pang of anxiety. Were they making a mistake and heading into danger? But Grimalkin had a mind of her own, and she was strong. She made her own decisions and who was I to try and interfere?

I went back up the steps and left the house, walking quickly towards the nearest of the standing stones. As soon as I was beyond them, the baleful red sky gave way once more to stars.

I didn't go far and as it was a warm pleasant June night I made myself comfortable on a grassy bank and didn't wake until dawn.

I used the daylight hours to explore Keswick's narrow cobbled streets and the surrounding countryside and had a good lunch at the Stag's Head tavern. I didn't bother with an evening meal despite my growing appetite. Like most spooks before me I preferred to face the dark with an empty stomach.

At dusk I approached the stones once more, and was soon waiting at their outer edge. After about an hour, when Grimalkin and Thorne didn't emerge from the circle, I became impatient and stepped within it. But the sky did not change. Where the strange house had stood were now just a few foundation stones.

The underworld had ceased to exist.

5

THE THREAT OF TORTURE

I did not give up easily and stayed another three days, determined to find Grimalkin and Thorne, but each late June evening, when dark fell, nothing had changed.

I tried summoning Thorne, attempting it several times each night. But there was never a silver sphere floating down towards me, no girl grinning a greeting.

I was now very worried about the witch assassins, and wished I had insisted that they'd returned to the dark in their usual manner. Anything could have happened to them in those tunnels. Had they encountered the tulpar whose lair this had been? And how powerful was that entity?

There was nothing further to be done here as I could not re-enter the underworld, so I decided to return to Chipenden but visit Silverdale again on my way back. I wanted to take another more careful look at that house and the black coach without windows.

When I arrived in Silverdale, I found things to be exactly as I had feared. There was no coach, just a heap of dust on the flags. The horses also had ceased to be. The only trace of them was the slime that coated the floor of the stables. All of this had been the work of a very skilful tulpar who had destroyed his creations and then left. Why go through with such an elaborate plan?

I set off walking south again, keeping to the left bank of the Caster canal for the major part of my journey – and as before I occasionally became Piddle and used the little dog's olfactory skills to sniff for danger. No doubt water witches were not too far away and I didn't want to be caught by a surprise attack.

Piddle sniffed out no water witches but he did find something else.

As I was approaching Caster, he detected another scent. It was that of the witch and her dog familiar that I'd encountered in the lakeside tavern. There was little that I could do about Thorne and Grimalkin but wait for them to make contact – so I decided to carry out a little spook's business now. It was likely that the witch was doing harm somewhere so it was my job to follow her to her lair to deal with the problem. Whatever else was going on, I was still the Chipenden Spook and that meant I had responsibilities to the County and beyond it.

I followed the trail of the witch and her familiar. It led me southeast towards another county – the one known as Yorkshire.

The route first took me through a large, picturesque village called Kirkby Lonsdale. I'd never visited it before but I had been reading some of Tom Ward's notebooks recently, slowly working my way through them. In the first one he wrote after becoming the Chipenden Spook, there was a detailed account of a visit here and how he had dealt with a ghost called Miriam, sending her to the light. Later in that book he'd also taken on an apprentice called Jenny – the first female ever to fill that role. I had met her once on leaving the dark and learned that she was the seventh daughter of a seventh daughter and a descendant of a mysterious people called the Samhadre, who were able to be reborn. She had died as a result of an attack by a water witch that had occurred along the bank of the canal I had just walked. Her passing had affected Tom badly.

So how had Jenny, that dead apprentice, managed to then go on to be in the company of the aged Tom and Alice who I had talked with in Hrothgar's lair?

I walked down the main street of the village, and following the sudden sharp left turn approached the Sun Inn where Tom had stayed to deal with its ghost all those years ago. I didn't want a room for the night but was really hungry and fancied a little more than a nibble of crumbly

County cheese, so I bought a satisfying roast lunch and then continued on my way following the trail of the witch, trying to keep thoughts of the witch assassins out of my mind.

Once again it was a pleasant day with June warmth in the sun, weather far removed from what I imagined the County was now experiencing, and long before dusk I settled myself down sheltering under a coppice of trees that edged the trail.

I decided to sleep in the form of the boy apprentice.

I couldn't resist trying again, calling out, 'Thorne!'

She did not respond to my summons and my worry for her and Grimalkin increased even more.

Because of this, sleep was a long time coming, my thoughts for them mixed in with those of the County. How far had its weather deteriorated by now? Was it already under a blanket of snow? If so, the crops would not be harvested and there would be a real threat of famine before the end of the year.

I awoke suddenly in the dawn light, feeling that something was very wrong. I was immediately very angry at myself for sleeping in the open so carelessly.

I was surrounded by six armed soldiers and they did not look friendly.

On second glance they did not seem much of a threat. There were two boys hardly older than I'd been when I had first become a monk; three grizzled veterans, too old to fight in a war; and a moustached sergeant, their leader, the only really capable warrior of the bunch. They wore uniforms: black woollen jackets and green hempen trousers with black leather boots. Each one carried a spear but the sergeant also had a sword in a scabbard at his belt.

'Well, what do we have here? A young spook if I'm not mistaken!' growled the sergeant. 'Search his bag!' he commanded and the two boys hastened to obey. He dragged me to my feet and gripped me by the hair, forcing my head back to expose my neck. Then he smiled and drew his sword. From his expression and the cruel look in his green eyes, it was hard to tell whether he intended to cut my throat or take me prisoner.

Now feeling in real danger, I was about to change into the warrior when one of the boys tugged the silver chain from my bag.

Immediately the sergeant's expression turned to one of greed. 'Don't all spooks have two silver chains?' he asked. 'Where's the other one?'

What he said wasn't true. Such chains were very expensive and a young spook was lucky to have one of his own. It usually took him years of hard work, saving carefully to purchase such a useful weapon. But the idea of two chains was one of those myths that people believed about spooks.

However, in my case it actually was true. I had inherited two chains from Tom Ward – the ones bequeathed to him by his own master, John Gregory.

'My other chain is back where I live,' I replied truthfully. 'In the next county.'

The sergeant smiled and sheathed his sword. 'Then it's best you come with us to the castle. My master will want to know all about you. Once he's got what he wants you'll be taking your last walk – back to your hovel so we can get the rest of what we need. Do you own any books, boy? My master loves books. He can never get enough!'

'Lots,' I told him. 'I have a whole library.'

'Then we'll need a cart. But first to Skipton Castle so you can have a little chat with my master!'

Of course, I could still have changed into the warrior tulpa. At which point, all six would have been lucky to take two more breaths before they died. But I couldn't do that. I could tell that the boys and the veterans were basically good people just following orders and afraid to refuse any command. The sergeant was something else but I saw no reason to kill him if it could be avoided. So I took a deep breath, kept calm and walked with them towards the castle. Escaping later would likely be easy enough.

As we travelled, the day gradually grew warmer and their woolly jackets made them sweat badly. It was hard to keep a smile from my face at their discomfort and I didn't feel I was in the slightest danger.

How wrong I was!

I wasn't walking as fast as they wanted.

'Faster, boy!' growled the sergeant. 'Haven't got all day!'

He was starting to irritate me, so I slowed my pace a little more, simply to be awkward.

For that I got a couple of painful jabs in the back from the spears of two of the veterans.

That made no difference to the speed of my progress and it wasn't long before the sergeant called a halt and gave me an evil smile. 'Hold your hands in front of you!' he barked at me. I did as he said but slightly apart. 'Palm against palm!' he snapped and I obeyed again.

Then I saw that he held a pair of metal handcuffs connected by a short chain which he slipped onto my wrists. I didn't see a key, but I heard a double click and knew that they were locked. They were too tight and quite painful, nipping my skin.

'Right, lads! He doesn't want to walk so let's drag him there!' He pushed me in the chest hard, taking me by surprise, and I fell over backwards. The two young soldiers came forward, quick to obey. Each grabbed me by a foot and began to drag me along the grass.

I writhed and struggled as the path changed and became narrower, the trees crowding in on either side. Roots broke the surface and the friction against my back became painful. Even worse, my head began to bang on them painfully. I'd had enough; I would change into the warrior. I'd use minimum violence but I was now determined to escape.

But when I tried to shift my shape into another tulpa, nothing happened.

I tried again but there was no response. Something was preventing the change. What could it be? It must be the cuffs. Did they contain some sort of powerful dark magic? Who were these people?

'I'll walk faster!' I shouted, after my head had made painful contact with a hard tree root once again.

The sergeant nodded to the two young soldiers and they dragged me to my feet. Then I walked faster as I had promised, but I was still cuffed. After an hour or so, we left the trees, followed a track through some farmland fields and entered the edge of what appeared to be quite a large busy town. This must be Skipton.

The castle was built on a hill overlooking closely packed dwellings and it was large and impressive. I expected it to be the opulent residence of a local lord.

It was only when we were beyond the portcullis, and it had dropped into position with a clang, that I realized my mistake. Although the walls were sound enough, viewed from within the courtyard the castle was mostly a ruin and looked to be uninhabited. I was pushed through a wooden door and found myself on spiral steps leading steeply downwards where it was difficult to keep my footing with my hands cuffed.

Then we were walking along dark underground passageways and passing through what seemed a labyrinth of small linked empty rooms until we reached a large door. The sergeant beat upon it three times with his fist.

'Enter!' boomed a voice and the door opened, then I was pushed through the entrance into the beginning of a nightmare. Inside seated at a large table was a quisitor – a big man, dressed in the long black gown of a priest. I'd met one before, and knew this was his torture chamber. I had been in one previously, in the days when I had first worked with Spook Johnson. That grim chamber contained many of the same horrors that I'd encountered before – a tray with a collection of instruments: spikes, sharp knives, pins and hooks, and pliers for extracting teeth and breaking fingers.

There were glass jars on the table too, which were full of various horrible items floating in cloudy liquids to preserve them and terrify future victims: teeth, eyeballs, tongues and fingers. There was also a larger jar full of ears sawn or cut from their victims' heads.

The Quisitor didn't bother to look at me but ordered the sergeant to tie me to a chair.

'I won't flee – there's no need to tie me!' I tried.

But I was quickly bound tightly with ropes round my legs, upper arms and chest. I noted that the chair was bolted to the flagged floor.

The sergeant made his report, doing it quickly and efficiently. He presented his master with my staff, bag and silver chain, informing him that I had a second one back at my home in the next county and he'd be pleased to be sent to retrieve it. He also mentioned that I had a large library and if he took horses and a cart he'd bring as many books as they could load back to the castle.

'Not only that,' he added with a sly grin, 'but if we take a cart, you won't need to be too kind to him. It won't matter whether he's capable of walking or not, will it?'

The Quisitor nodded and smiled at the sergeant, then gestured with his hand and the six soldiers left the room, closing the door quietly behind them.

He walked over and looked down at me. 'Not many of your kind left, are there?' he gloated. 'You're only the second one I've dealt with in five years.'

I was surprised he'd even met another spook. As far as I could be sure, I was the only one working within the County. Beyond its boundaries, there could well be more but I knew nothing of them.

'Witches are my priority but I know a lot about spooks by now,' he said. 'I'm familiar with their practices and their sinful interference in the proper business of the Holy Church. So what I want from you is the location of your spook brethren. I'm going to hurt you badly anyway, because you're ungodly and deserve punishment – but we could perhaps lessen your pain to some degree if you first tell me what I most need to hear. Tell me about all the other spooks of your acquaintance and where they are to be found.'

'There was a spook called Tom Ward and another who went by the name of Spook Johnson,' I replied. 'I met them both and worked with them but by now they are long dead. I know of no living spooks!'

'You're a difficult boy to read,' the Quisitor said, taking a step closer. 'I cannot tell whether you are lying or not. So I have to make sure, and only the most severe pain that I can inflict might loosen your tongue. I've devised certain effective techniques to prise the truth from witches and spooks. I favour what I like to call a crescendo of pain – a degree of extreme discomfort that gradually increases until a climax of agony is attained which is unbearable.'

He reached into a pocket and pulled out a pinch of snuff between his finger and thumb. This he sucked up into his nostrils with a loud snort, before sighing contentedly and then dabbing at his nose with a mottled handkerchief, removing only about half of the brown discolouration from his skin. Then he walked across to the table and returned holding a small pair of pliers. 'I'll just pull out a couple of your fingernails to get things started, then I'll turn my attention to your eyes. I'm sure you'll be able to manage with only one of them . . .'

Instantly all my courage drained from me. I was terrified, but refused to let it show, controlling my shaking. Pain received in battle was one thing – hurt when in the shape of the sky wolf or the warrior was something I could easily cope with. I'd been badly wounded before and fighting the battle held my full attention, meaning I hardly noticed the pain until afterwards. But this was different. The thought of being restrained and passive while being tortured was unbearable.

The Quisitor stepped forward and seized my left hand in a firm grip. But instantly he let it go.

I looked up at him in astonishment. From somewhere behind me, a spook's staff had been driven with extreme force over my shoulder and deep into the Quisitor's forehead, the blade buried into him up to the hilt.

But there was no surge of blood from the wound. Instead, he seemed to shiver; both his shoulders twitched and then he fell to his knees. Then he began to fall apart, his face sliding down onto his chest, his flesh becoming clay and dust.

I was watching the end of another tulpa. The deceptions continued around me. As the tulpa was reduced to a pile of slime and rags on the floor, the bearer of the staff walked round to face me.

It was a girl I knew. One who wore the garb of a spook. The girl who had been Tom Ward's apprentice.

It was Jenny Calder.

Without speaking, Jenny pulled a knife from her belt and began to cut the rope that bound me to the chair. I came to my feet as she knelt and began to rummage in the slime and rags that had once been the Quisitor.

Then she smiled and held up a small key which she quickly used to free me from the handcuffs. 'Let's get out of here, Wulf. The soldiers aren't tulpas and I don't want to have to harm them. They're busy drinking ale at the moment so we could be long gone before they realize what's happened.' She saw I was about to speak. 'Explanations later – you do remember me, don't you? My name's Jenny. I was trained by Tom Ward but that was another me. I remember you.'

I nodded, aware of her ability to be reborn. 'I certainly do remember you, Jenny, and thanks for intervening,' I said. 'I was careless to get caught like that.'

'You were never in any real danger,' she told me, walking away from me towards the door. 'I've been following you since you left Kirkby Lonsdale.'

'Why?' I asked, annoyed with myself that I hadn't spotted her at any point. 'Why were you following me?'

'It's a long story!' she replied with a cheeky grin. 'I'll tell you later – once we're clear of this place.'

We had no problems in leaving the castle, seeing nothing of the sergeant and his men. The one locked door we encountered I solved in seconds by changing my shape to that of Saint Quentin, who found the lock no impediment at all, and it was easy enough to raise the portcullis.

Soon we had left Skipton and its castle far behind and were walking through the trees, retracing the steps I'd taken as a prisoner.

'I'm hoping to pick up the trail of a witch,' I told Jenny. 'I've been following her for a while. That's what took me through Kirkby Lonsdale.'

'Do you mind if I stay with you for a bit? I might be able to help.'

'You're welcome to do that,' I told her. 'But first I've a few questions I'd like to ask you.'

So as we walked, I was straightforward about what was bothering me. How could she be the same Jenny that I had met over a century ago? And if she wasn't that Jenny – then what was she?

She didn't answer my question but came to a halt and glared at me. 'Alice and Tom called me out like this when I came back last time. They really thought that I was a gristle and that calling me that would prove that and destroy me!'

'You are a tulpa!' I cried with a wicked grin. 'Writhe in agony and crumble into dust! Slough off your false flesh and turn into stinky slime!'

Of course, nothing happened. She *was* Jenny and her attitude had already convinced me of that fact. But she scowled and clearly didn't appreciate my little joke!

'What's wrong?' I demanded. 'Your face is twisted as if you'd just sucked a bitter plum!'

'What you said was cruel!' Jenny asserted. 'Don't you know how terrible it is for a gristle to learn the truth about itself and then dissolve into oblivion?'

'Of course I know!' I snapped back. 'I would never create a human gristle for that very reason. I knew you weren't a tulpa. It was only a joke!'

'Well, you have a strange sense of humour!' she said. 'So, from now on keep your silly jokes to yourself and we might get on better!'

'We don't need to get on, because there's no reason for us to be in each other's company,' I told her. I didn't like her attitude. 'Thank you for rescuing me, but now we need to part. I have things to do and your presence will slow me down.'

'Oh! You really don't want to get rid of me, Wulf! You won't last very long without *my* help.'

'You have a false sense of your own importance!' I told her angrily.

'Do I? Well then, let me tell you a few home truths. All those years ago, I wanted Tom Ward to take me on as his apprentice but he kept refusing. He was exactly like you.

Because I was a girl, he didn't see my worth. In the end I had to prove to him exactly what I could do. He'd been trying to hunt down a dangerous creature – without much success. He was getting nowhere. I was the one who found its lair and led him there so that eventually he managed to destroy it. That's because I can find things that others can't and I can go places unseen that others can't. That means I *know* things that other people don't know – even experienced spooks. Even you, Wulf!'

I'd had enough of her boasting. I changed into the tulpa of the sky wolf and soared aloft without even looking at her. Another second and I'd have been away, high into the sky and far beyond the range of her irritating voice.

As it was, I just about heard what she cried out.

'I know who the enemy of Pan is! I know the name of *your* enemy – the one who wants to become the new ruler of the dark!'

6

MOTHER SHIPTON

'This had better not be a trick!' I warned her. 'If you *really* know the name of my enemy, then tell me now!' I had flown down and changed back into the form of the warrior to stand directly before her.

Jenny grinned. 'Where shall I start? Which name should I begin with? Because there's no shortage of names. This could take quite some time! I'm hungry and I think you should feed me first.'

'I'll feed you,' I told her. 'Then you need to tell me everything. How did you find me? How did you know I was passing through Kirkby Lonsdale?'

'My nose is more sensitive than even most witches can manage and you were pretty easy to sniff out – you need to change your socks more frequently!' she said, grinning at me cheekily.

Despite myself, I smiled back.

It was dark now, and the sky was full of bright stars, the air warm – it was a pleasant summer night. We sat facing each other across a small fire, both of us licking our fingers to savour the last of the tasty rabbits that we'd just been eating.

'Begin at the beginning and leave nothing out!' I was stern across the embers. 'Start with the name of my enemy.'

'Yes, master!' she said in a mocking voice. 'Well, your enemy has many names because, as one of the most ancient of the Old Gods, he's been worshipped in many different locations and has taken on a multitude of guises. In the far north he was one of the Norse gods and went by the name of Loki, although a lot of humans called him the Trickster God. And that takes us right to the very heart of him – he likes to fool folks and play games. Nothing gives him greater pleasure.

'In another guise he is known as Trigor where he takes on the form of a green three-eyed demon. I met him in my last lifetime although I didn't know it at the time because he'd taken on another shape – that of a boy minstrel.'

I'd seen the three-eyed demon during the battle in the valley close to Chipenden but he'd escaped my clutches. Had that been this Trigor?

'There's a whole list of aspects he's been known and worshipped under but I'll leave them until after I've explained about the worst one of them all – the one that directly concerns you, Wulf! He was once known as the Maker. He made creatures out of clay and sent them to walk the earth. The stories around him were that if you prayed hard enough, he would give you back your lost loved one – return a family member who had died to you. They *seemed* to be exactly the same as the person that you'd lost but there was one big drawback. If the creature ever found out that they were a replacement and not the real human, they dissolved into slime and rags and that was the end of them!'

'Then they were tulpas!' I exclaimed in astonishment. 'They were gristles!'

'That's exactly what they were! And now it gets even worse. Some believe that Loki was the god of tulpars – that he had children by human women and his power passed down into the human race. That means *your* power to create tulpas could well have come down to you through his bloodline, Wulf. You might well be one of his descendants! That might also make it very hard for you to defeat him. Don't you see? He has the same type of talent that you have, but because he's a god he will be infinitely better at it and much more powerful.'

I gazed into the embers, letting the enormity of what Jenny was telling me sink into my head. The Latin inscription over the door of that strange building in the stone circle swirled around my head.

Eagles Do Not Breed Doves . . .

Was Loki trying to tell me that I was his son? Of course, I was not his son in human terms, but maybe his blood still flowed through my veins. If so and he had my abilities, the same but far superior to mine, how could I hope to defeat him? And I thought about the tulpa quisitor. Had Loki created him? Had he also created the Tom and Alice that I'd encountered? Was he playing games with me? Why?

I told Jenny about the coach that had been used to confine and transport Grimalkin and how Thorne and I had rescued her from the Tom and Alice tulpas. I told her of the disappearance of the witch assassin and Thorne – everything that I'd experienced recently.

When I'd finished, she simply said, 'You need my help, and would be stupid to refuse it.'

I nodded, feeling chastened. 'Thanks for what you've told me, Jenny. Your help would be much appreciated. I need time to think and plan. And so while I do that we might as well get back on the trail of that witch and her familiar. I'm still the Chipenden Spook but I warn you, Jenny, if you want to be my apprentice then forget it. I don't have the time to train you properly.'

Jenny laughed loudly and shook her head. 'I don't want to be anybody's apprentice!' she declared. 'In my last lifetime I completed an apprenticeship with Tom Ward. Then I spent over another thirty years practising that trade. Compared with me and my experience as a spook, you are just a beginner! *You* could be *my* apprentice but I'm sorry, *I* don't have the time to train *you* properly! And that explains why I'm here now looking no older than when you last saw me. We Samhadre die but then are born again as children. So here I am!'

I held up my hand to admit my mistake then stared into the embers of the fire again, trying to digest all that she'd told me. It was a while before either of us spoke again.

'Were you with Tom and Alice until they died?' I asked. I wanted to ask about Tilda too, but stopped myself.

Jenny shook her head. 'Tom wanted me to take over at Chipenden but I got the wanderlust and went on my travels. He was disappointed but accepted my decision. When I went back many years later, I found the three graves. I'd expected Tom's and Alice's as they were getting on in years when I left but Tilda's was a real surprise. She would still have been relatively young, so I don't know how she met her end or who buried her. Nobody down in the village knew anything about it. And now so much time has passed by that we'll never find out. Sorry I can't tell you more, Wulf. I know that you and Tilda were very close. Tom and Alice waited almost a year before they finally left Hrothgar's lair because Tilda wouldn't give up on you. They practically had to drag her back to Chipenden. She kept saying you'd come back and, of course, she was eventually proved to be right.'

'Yes,' I answered sadly. 'But too late. I fought the Fiend and although I won it was almost the end of me. While I was in the dark recovering, so much time passed back on earth. Pan cured me but he always charges a high price for his services. Now I serve him and fight against other creatures of the dark on his behalf.'

'Against Loki then?'

I nodded. 'If this is all him and he wants to be the ruler of the dark, that's the latest threat that Pan will have me deal with, yes.'

'Then no doubt that's why Loki is taking a special interest in you.'

'It could be,' I admitted.

'But he's not killed you, has he? He's playing with you or maybe he's testing you to see what you can really do. He would have created the quisitor and also provided the cuffs that took away your ability to change your shape. As I said, he likes to play games and what could be better than to fight and tease someone with similar but inferior abilities to his own.'

I nodded. The more Jenny said, the worse it sounded.

'Don't look so glum, Wulf. There'll be a way to beat him. They call him the Trickster God – well, maybe we can think up a few tricks of our own!'

I sighed. 'Out-trick the Trickster God. That would be something, wouldn't it!'

'Why not? Imagination is the key to what you do, isn't it? Well, he may be a god and more powerful than you in many ways but there is no certainty that his imagination is more powerful than yours. After all, you're human and sometimes humans have an advantage over the Old Gods – they've existed too long and are rigid in their thinking and set in their ways. Whereas human lives are brief, and their minds can be more agile. And Loki has me to reckon with too, hasn't he? I'm not human. I'm one of the Samhadre, the Old Ones, the Faery Folk, and we've fought the Old Gods before and sometimes given out a few bloody noses! It's me and you, Wulf, against a common enemy. The bigger they are the harder they fall. Working together, we can bring Loki tumbling down!'

I smiled at her. She was so bubbly and confident – it was an antidote for the way I was feeling.

Soon after that we settled down on opposite sides of the fire and went to sleep.

*

I was woken early by the dawn light. Jenny was already awake. 'Shall we pick up the witch's trail and breakfast later?' she asked.

I nodded and we set off. I had no need to change into the Piddle tulpa with Jenny here – she soon picked up the scent of our quarry. Late in the afternoon we were walking along the banks of a wide river. Ahead was the arch of a low bridge. As we stepped within its shadows Jenny reached for my arm in silence. I knew that the witch was not too far ahead. And she wasn't moving. It seemed likely that we'd found her lair.

I gripped my staff, nodding towards the thicket of trees on the bank of the river. 'She's somewhere in there?'

'I'll go ahead and take a look,' Jenny suggested. 'I promise that I'll do nothing alone. We'll deal with her together. But I can get close without her seeing me. Once I know how the land lies, I'll come back.'

I could see no harm in that; it sounded like a smart idea. Jenny could make herself as good as invisible – I'd seen that talent for myself when she'd appeared out of nowhere and dealt with the tulpa quisitor.

Jenny placed her bag and staff on the ground next to me and I waited in the shadows beneath the bridge and watched her walk slowly forward towards the trees. The late-afternoon sun was shining brightly out of a clear blue sky without a cloud in sight and I could see Jenny's shadow on the grass behind her. That was the first part of her to disappear. Then there was a quick shimmer and she seemed to vanish altogether, completely blending into the trees as she approached.

It was about five minutes before she returned, striding rapidly across the grass towards me. She pointed in the direction we'd come from, but when I opened my mouth to question her she frowned then placed her forefinger vertically against her lips to insist upon silence.

I was annoyed at being told what to do, but she strode by picking up her staff and bag as she passed me, giving me no choice but to turn on my heels and follow her. She didn't stop until we were at least a mile further on down the riverbank.

We sat on the grass facing each other. 'It's bad,' she told me. 'Actually, the situation couldn't be worse!'

'Did the witch know you were there?' I asked, listening to the water gurgling over the stones close to the bank.

Jenny shook her head. 'She didn't detect *me* but she knew that you were lurking nearby.'

'You can read minds then, as well as making yourself invisible!'

'I wish I could. I only know because she talks aloud to herself as well as to her familiar. But – that's the point, she's not a true witch and that isn't a real familiar. They're both tulpas.'

I was surprised. 'You're sure about that?'

'I might not be able to read minds but I do know a tulpa when I'm close to it. That's one of my gifts.'

'Then when you dealt with the quisitor, why didn't you name him rather than slay him with your staff?'

'He was about to hurt you badly. Had I called him out, there might have been time enough for him to harm you before he disintegrated. Using the blade of my staff was faster and more certain.'

I nodded. 'So, why is the situation so bad?' I asked. 'We can walk into her lair and name her as a tulpa. Then it will be over.'

'This witch tulpa is a bit different,' Jenny said. 'We *could* name her but she might destroy us first. She's dangerous, Wulf. I could sense the magic pouring out of her. Her lair is a cave and there's also dark magical power stored in the rocks – a lot of power. The real witch was slain long ago and is buried under an elm tree further down the bank. But this tulpa has all her powers and maybe more. Loki must have made her specially for you. This could be his final trap – she's a serious threat. Maybe he got bored with playing tricks and wants to finish you off?'

'So, you're suggesting that we just walk away? As a spook it's my duty to protect the folk who live in this area.'

'I'm a spook too! And this gristle is no threat to the locals. Loki has created it to confront *you*! The original witch was called Mother Shipton and she seemed to do little harm apart from scare folk occasionally. Her talent was prophecy. She wrote a popular book describing things that'll happen far into the future. But she had another book, a special one that few people ever saw. In it she wrote down things that she *caused* to happen in the future using her dark magic. For a price paid by a desperate wife, she would cause a violent husband to fall from a ladder and break his neck. What she wrote into that book seemed to happen.'

'How do you know all this?' I asked. 'Did you deal with Mother Shipton?'

Jenny shook her head. 'She was hunted down and killed by Spook Johnson. And he was the one who buried her under that tree. Then he made himself scarce because she was quite popular in these parts. Nobody knew she was dead – probably thought she'd gone off travelling – and so her return hasn't caused much surprise. Loki has gone to a lot of trouble to put that gristle here to do you harm. She might already have used Mother Shipton's special book. She might have written down how you die. Where did you first encounter her?'

'I was north of Windermere heading towards Keswick to find Grimalkin. I was hungry so I called into a tavern to get a bite to eat. She was there with what I thought was her child. Later, on my way back, I picked up her trail again . . .'

'And that was the beginning of the trap. It was no coincidence that she was in that tavern. She was there waiting for you!'

'So what do you suggest?'

'We need to head back towards Chipenden. Why face her in that cave where she's surrounded by extra magic that she can draw upon? If we leave, she'll follow us. It'll be easier to deal with two gristles out in the open.'

7

THE PROPHECY

Jenny reminded me of Tilda in that she was a force to be reckoned with. If you weren't careful either of them was more than capable of taking the lead and making you move in the direction that they wanted. A part of me resented that. I was confident that I could deal with the tulpa witch and her familiar on my own. I could see the wisdom of not entering the cave but, rather than retreat towards Chipenden pursued by my enemies, I favoured waiting here and attacking the moment they emerged. They couldn't stay in that cave forever.

But I took a deep breath and swallowed my pride. 'OK then, we'll head back towards Chipenden. I just hope that you're right and she follows us.'

'She will!' said Jenny with her cheeky grin. 'And with her familiar gristle at her heels.'

Five minutes later we were on our way back to the spook's house at Chipenden, walking at a brisk pace.

As we approached the County, the visible change was dramatic. Ahead, on its border, was a line of leafless trees, their bare branches stark against the sky. As we walked beneath them, the temperature dropped alarmingly. One moment it had been a warm but windy June evening. The next it was as cold as January. Things here had got much worse while I had been away.

It seemed that Loki was powerful enough to seize and control the weather of the County despite all that Pan could do. For surely the God of Nature would not allow this if he were free to return the weather here to its normal patterns? Of course, Loki would have lots of help in what he was doing. Each time that an Old God tried to become dominant and rule the dark, they needed supporters. This was usually an alliance of demons and Old Gods like themselves. No doubt Golgoth, the Lord of Winter, was playing a very important role here in support of Loki.

We didn't halt until dusk. I left Jenny to make a fire then I changed into the sky wolf and soared aloft. The sky was darkening but still I took no chances over being seen. I flew very high so that from below I would have been no more than a faint speck in the sky.

As the sky wolf my eyes were incredibly keen and they soon confirmed that Jenny was right. The witch gristle *was* following us, her small dog familiar loping at her heels. The sky wolf liked taking risks and, despite the unknown dangers presented by the gristles below, was eager to attack. But I'd promised Jenny that we would confront the danger together and so I forced myself back to her.

'It'll take them about two hours to reach here,' I told Jenny, watching her on her knees teasing the fire into life. She was shivering. It really was as cold as I'd ever known it.

She looked up and smiled at me. 'That's long enough for us to grab some supper. I'm hungry, so why don't you go off and catch us a couple of rabbits?'

I was hungry too and could have changed back into the sky wolf and caught and eaten my prey raw. But, once more, I did what Jenny suggested – though I worried she might be getting too used to me following her orders! I hunted for rabbits to take back, cook and share. There were plenty of the creatures around. Rabbits didn't hibernate but switched their diet to bark and conifer needles in the winter. Within fifteen minutes or so, two rabbits were caught, skinned and gutted and now Jenny was turning them on a spit while I warmed my hands.

'You should let me deal with that witch gristle,' said Jenny. 'After all, it seems pretty obvious that the threat is to you. It can sense you but not me. I could take it by surprise. You can have the familiar.'

'That does makes sense,' I said agreeably.

But what I said didn't quite match my thoughts. If Loki truly was a trickster, we could expect an unpleasant surprise – maybe more than one. Who knows what might await us . . .

As we walked to meet our enemies, the moon rose slowly above the leafless trees. Its silver light would make a surprise attack more difficult – but not for Jenny. I waited in the shadows while she made the first approach.

I watched as she appeared very suddenly, bathed in silver light, just one stride away from the witch and taking her completely by surprise.

Her attack was perfectly executed. Using the method that she'd used to slay the quisitor tulpa, Jenny drove the silver blade of her staff straight into the forehead of the witch. The creature gave a loud gasp and fell to its knees. By which time I had already left the shadows and was running straight at the dog familiar – but it was already racing towards Jenny, its mouth wide open, fangs bared. It looked larger than before, the size of an adult wolf.

I intercepted it and, using my staff, drove the blade straight into the back of the tulpa's neck, pinning it to the ground.

That should have been the end of both gristles, but I had been right. The Trickster God had his first unpleasant surprise ready for us. Before the creatures began to dissolve back into slime, their heads suddenly burst, expanding into two dark liquid clouds.

I jumped back, narrowly avoiding being splattered from head to foot. Even so, some of the dark material landed on my boots and trousers, small black blobs of what appeared to be slime. And as I pulled my staff free, I instinctively brushed the mess away.

Then there was the next shock. The small blobs were moving. They had legs!

By then Jenny had reached my side. 'They're tiny spiders!' she cried, stamping on as many as she could as they scurried away into the grass to be hidden from our sight.

I squashed what I could before they left my breeches and boots, but some got away. Warnings were going off inside my head fed by my own knowledge of tulpas. These spider-things were tulpas that could grow.

They were surely the weapons of Loki, a god who had my abilities and skills but to a much more advanced degree. I couldn't have created a gristle that could break into smaller entities. But I did have one hope. Gristles needed energy – food. To grow and become a truly dangerous threat would take these creatures some time.

So I gripped Jenny's arm. 'Run!'

Jenny paused to snatch up her bag, then she bent and picked up something else from the pool of slime. There was no time now for me to ask what.

We set off towards Chipenden as though hordes of demons were at our heels. After about ten minutes we slowed to a jog and continued at the same pace for almost four hours. Then, just before dawn, we rested and I explained my fears.

'But they're really small and they'll surely need to eat a *lot* of food to grow, won't they?' she asked, her calculation of the situation the same as mine.

'Yes, and that should slow them down.'

'Can they eat vegetation?'

'All the gristles that Hrothgar and I created needed meat to sustain them. Prey will be hard to find but I don't think we can rule it out completely. Though even if these gristles are different, most of the vegetation is dead too, killed by the unseasonal cold,' I said, looking around at the denuded trees and ground about us.

We set off again at a brisk walking pace, and by mid-morning we'd reached the Chipenden house.

'I feel safe here,' said Jenny.

I knew what she meant. The boggart gave one loud warning howl then, recognizing us, moved away into the trees. Although now blinded in both eyes, the consequences of fighting off dangerous intruders in the past, it was still formidable. I believed that, whatever the size and number of the spider tulpas, if they attacked, the boggart would make short work of them.

And even if I was greatly underestimating the threat they posed, we would still receive warning howls from the boggart. We'd certainly not be taken by surprise. Yes, *I* felt safe at Chipenden too.

Feeling that sense of security and both of us exhausted, we slept through the remainder of the daylight hours. I went to my usual bedroom, the one taken by generations of apprentices, while Jenny slept in the bedroom once used by John Gregory.

The following morning, after a delicious breakfast cooked by the boggart, Jenny placed a small book on the kitchen table.

'This is what I grabbed from the slime yesterday. It's Mother Shipton's book which creates prophecies that come true,' Jenny said. 'I've read some of them and they're quite nasty. A husband falling from an apple tree and breaking his neck so that his wife was free to re-marry; a village burning down during a thunderstorm so that the local landowner could clear the tenants from his land and replace them with sheep. And there is one for you. Wulf . . .'

'Tell me the worst.'

Jenny opened the book, about to read the prophecy to me. Then she shook her head sadly and pushed the book across the table towards me, using her thumb to keep it open at the right page.

I read aloud:

'Brother Beowulf shall die in a citadel of ice owned by Lord Golgoth. No human will be at his side and demons will swarm around his place of execution. He will first be tortured and die in great pain.'

I laughed aloud, closed the book and slid it back towards her across the table.

Jenny shook her head sadly. 'I know you're trying to be brave, Wulf, but this is a book of prophecies that come true.'

'We'll see about that!' I countered. 'Nothing is fixed in this world. When a witch scries and foretells what *seems* to be the future, it's changing even as she speaks. The future is *never* fixed and is remade from moment to moment by the decisions and actions of us all. Thank you for bringing it to my attention, Jenny, but it doesn't scare me in the slightest. What will be will be but only because I will make it happen.'

We sat in silence for a while and then Jenny went to the fire and threw the book into the flames.

THE BATTLE OF CHIPENDEN

It was three days before the bell rang at midnight down at the withy trees crossroads.

We found a young boy there, the son of the village grocer. He looked no older than eight or nine and was tugging the rope frantically, terror twisting his face. When he saw us emerge from the hedge that bordered the garden, he ran across towards us sobbing with fear.

'Demons! Demons!' he cried, pointing down towards Chipenden.

'Describe what's happening,' I ordered.

'Demon beasts on long stick-thin legs!' he cried. 'Most folk have locked themselves in their houses. The beasts can be killed – the blacksmith battered one to death with his big hammer, squashing its head – but there are too many to fight! Help us! Please help us!'

'The creatures must be ready for us,' Jenny said grimly.

And without further delay, we ran down into the village at speed, leaving the boy far behind us as he struggled to keep up. It was a windy night with clouds surging in from Morecambe Bay, but there were plenty of areas of clear sky through which occasionally shone the silver light of the moon.

Soon we were running down the cobbled street that led towards the village centre. None of the houses were showing the gleam of candles and I wondered if the villagers had fled. A large cloud had blocked the moonlight and, in the darkness ahead, we were confronted by scores of red glowing eyes.

We came to a halt and Jenny and I prepared to fight.

Within moments the moon came out again, bathing the street in its silver light, and we saw our enemies properly.

I had thought the small pieces of slime that had burst from the heads of the witch and dog tulpas had been tiny insects, and Jenny had called them spiders. We had both been wrong.

They had grown rapidly and now I could see what the creatures truly were. The gristles were as tall as I was. Their bodies and heads were that of fearsome fanged cats, but each creature was balanced on six long, very thin black legs like those of an insect. Each triple-jointed leg ended in a long foot with three clawed toes. Those spindly legs quivered in excitement as they prepared to attack. I could hear the clicking of their joints and the scratching of their claws against the cobbles. They were horrible.

Their short-haired hides were patterned with distinctive ovals, brown on white, and their jaws were far larger and more threatening than those of domestic cats. They were similar to the illustrations of dangerous predatory felines in bestiaries that I'd seen back in the scriptorium at the abbey, waiting to be copied. I'd encountered such a creature before when I had entered the dark looking for Hrothgar. I had been in the shape of Piddle and the creature had stalked me until I had changed my tulpa, becoming Black Fang, a large wolf. I'd leaped at it and ripped out its throat.

I realized now that must have been my first encounter with a gristle created by Loki. He must have been observing and stalking me even then, beginning to play his games and tricks to gain control of the dark.

And now he had unleashed a horde of the creatures. He'd not sent them against the house, where the boggart would have defended the garden. Craftily, he had directed them against the village of Chipenden, which he knew it was my duty to defend. As I had suspected we might, Jenny and I had been lured out here in the open where we could be attacked and slain.

As I took on the form of the warrior, one of the nearest creature's legs suddenly twitched forward before it left the pack of gristles completely and ran towards me very fast, its jaws wide open with hunger, long fangs dripping saliva. The warrior was better with a sword than a staff but I had practised hard with both to hone my skills.

I swept the staff sideways, keeping it low. The silver-alloy blade cut through the gristle's front legs, bringing it toppling forward. Before it hit the ground, my blade had pierced its skull and it immediately shuddered and began to dissolve into slime.

'The next one's mine!' cried Jenny.

'You're spoilt for choice!'

The creatures covered the width of the street, blocking our way entirely, and many more waited behind. Rank upon rank of them faced us, predatory eyes gleaming in the starlight, legs trembling with the anticipation of feeding upon our flesh.

I cast my staff down upon the cobbles. We had a difficult fight ahead. 'Sword!' I cried. There was a pleasing rasp as it dropped into the scabbard upon my back.

Shoulder to shoulder, Jenny and I could not control the full width of the main street with this many of them. There was a danger that the gristles would break through on either side and surround us. But they might not need to do that. There were narrow alleys intersecting with the main street. Some of those access points were behind us. They could use those and soon we'd have to fight back to back.

Suddenly there was a noise from the alley close on my left and I drew my sword and turned to face it. But it wasn't a gristle. A tall man strode towards us from the shadows. It was the blacksmith, a big hammer resting upon his right shoulder which he was gripping two-handed. Despite the cold he wore just a short-sleeved shirt as if straight from working at the forge, the muscles in his arms sharply defined.

'I've killed two,' he said, 'but both of them were alone. Now it looks like we've a real fight on our hands. But more help is on its way – some of the local farmers will be here soon!' He stared at me in my warrior form, wondering for a moment who I might be.

Before I could reply, the mass of gristles attacked. We turned to face them, Jenny on my right, the blacksmith on my left. Now we covered the full width of the street and, unless one of us fell, there was no way they could get past us.

The creatures' powerful, sleek predatory bodies advanced towards us, the bowed spindly legs that supported them seemingly unsuited for their task.

The smith was eager to fight and stepped forward to deliver a telling blow against one of our foes. He brought the huge hammer down from over his head in a fast accurate arc that battered a gristle to the ground, smearing its blood and brains into the cobbles. This big man was very brave. I knew that he was the great grandson of the blacksmith who'd been such a staunch ally of John Gregory back in the days when he'd been the County Spook. And he had done me service before, forging the iron bars needed to seal witches within their pits.

Out of the corner of my eye, I glimpsed Jenny stabbing her staff forward towards the head of the gristle now confronting her. Those thin quivering legs were stronger than they looked and suddenly their jointed curve straightened so that the gristle became much taller. One second Jenny was facing an enemy whose savage face was on the same level as her own; the next that countenance reared two feet above her and the hungry jaws snapped down towards the top of her skull.

Jenny's speed and skill with her staff saved her. She stepped back a pace and then thrust upwards, burying the blade in the left eye of her attacker.

Then I was forced to concentrate on my own opponent. In the shape of the warrior, I was fast and strong with rapid reflexes. I sliced the head of the gristle from its body, which I stepped over to attack the next of the monsters before it could step into the gap. Then I checked my advance, waiting for the blacksmith and Jenny to fight their way forward to once more stand alongside me. We needed to hold a defensive line.

That became the pattern of the battle. One of us would gain ground on the others and then need to wait until they caught up and, once more, we all stood shoulder to shoulder. The blacksmith was skilful and impressive with his deadly use of that huge hammer and Jenny was using the staff with more skill than I could ever have managed. I was better off using my sword. I'd never completed my spook's training, whereas Jenny had lived a previous lifetime fighting as a spook against the dark and seemed to have retained everything that she had learned.

'Where are those farmers?' I yelled.

Grimly and without looking at me the blacksmith shook his head. 'No idea. They should have been just behind me.'

Bit by bit, stroke by stroke, we began to drive our enemies back. Soon so many had fallen that it was their dead bodies that became a hindrance, causing us to step forward very carefully, each dead tulpa taking longer and longer to dissolve into slime. But we were winning, there was no doubt about that, and now I could sense the fear rising from the creatures.

At last, they broke ranks and fled. The blacksmith told us that many of the villagers had taken refuge in the church with their children, so we left the main street and headed there.

I was fearful of what we would find. While we'd fought the mass of gristles, others might have forced their way into the church and slaughtered everyone inside. But there was no sign of gristles nearby and thankfully everyone was unharmed – the villagers had survived, albeit fearful and traumatized. Next to locate were the farmers who should have joined us in that desperate fight on the main street of Chipenden.

Soon, to our shock and dismay, we learned what had happened to them.

'Oh no!' Jenny yelped, catching sight of something in one of the alleys.

'Good Lord.' This came from the smith.

I thought I knew what I would see before I joined them in seeing it.

It was worse.

There had been five in all, men brave enough to fight demons. With only pitchforks and clubs as weapons, they'd obviously made their way towards the main street to join the battle but had been intercepted and never reached us.

There was not much left of them. Three fathers and two sons.

Predatory gristles, those given the shapes of animals for combat, have a raging hunger. They feed upon their prey. Suddenly our victory seemed hollow.

Our battle wasn't even completed. The gristles that had fled the main street could not be allowed to remain at large in the County. They now needed to be hunted down and slain.

9

THE CHIPENDEN BOGGART

Piddle alone sniffed out every last gristle. We killed all but one, and soon tracked down the last one. The final creature was hiding in a churchyard, lurking high up within the gnarled branches of an ancient yew tree, the evergreen leaves offering a rare hiding place.

I changed into my wolf tulpa, Black Fang, leaped the gate and bounded between the gravestones, prepared to drive it from its refuge and slay it. But the gristle clambered down the trunk to confront me. In every respect but one it was the same as its fellows. It had the same six triple-jointed spindly legs and cat-like upper body. But its head was without fur, covered in grey skin and was human in shape. The eyes were still those of a cat but when it opened its mouth to reveal its fangs it spoke to me.

'You have proved yourself worthy!' it rasped.

I changed my form back into that of the warrior. 'Sword!' I cried and the weapon scraped into the scabbard on my back. I reached back and drew it and took a step towards the gristle, demanding angrily, 'Worthy of what?'

'Worthy to serve my master.'

'I serve nobody.'

'You serve Pan.'

'I serve nobody,' I repeated. 'Our aims are similar and we fight the same enemies.'

I had originally refused Pan when he'd demanded that I serve him. I had told the Old God that I would not be his servant. But his arguments had been persuasive. He would help me with his magic. I would fight the dark as had always been my intention. Was working together with the same aims not a sensible way forward? In alliance we could win our war against the worst aspects of the dark.

I had agreed. To deny that I served Pan was perhaps splitting hairs but we both profited from our alliance. He could not directly fight other deities. It was too dangerous and too many adversaries might align to destroy him. But Pan wanted to curb the worst of the dark by destroying those who aimed to create a Hell on earth. To achieve that, I was his instrument.

The gristle took a step towards me and I raised my sword ready to meet any attack.

'My master will not repeat this offer!' cried the gristle. 'He offers it because his blood circulates within you.'

What Jenny had worked out was true then. I was one of Loki's descendants. I pushed my repulsion aside.

'You are one of his creatures and it is part of the natural order of things that you serve him. Think carefully. Deliberate before giving me your answer.'

I deliberated for two seconds then I gave my answer.

The head of the gristle bounced once, then rolled across the grass, coming to a halt against a gravestone. It still stared at me for a while, its thin lips twitching into a mocking smile. Then it died, slime flowing away into the soggy ground.

I returned to Chipenden, and after thanking the blacksmith again, now back to my normal spook's appearance, Jenny and I climbed the hill back to the house. It was three in the morning but already there was a glow on the horizon to the east. Our breath steamed into the air. It would be another bitterly cold day. As we walked, I told Jenny about my successful hunt and the conversation that I'd had with the last of the gristles that I'd slain.

'The trickster will no longer play games with you,' said Jenny. 'He'll want to destroy you.'

I nodded. 'I'll take refuge in the house and fight him from there. There's no need for you to risk your life, Jenny. Be best if you went on your travels. You've helped me enough already.'

'You don't get rid of me that easily!' she replied. 'It's my fight now as well. But I'm not sure if it's a good idea to fight from the house.'

'Why not?' I asked.

'I'd prefer to keep moving – not stay in one place where Loki can gather his forces to use against us.'

'I take your point, Jenny, but the Chipenden house is an excellent place to endure a siege, one of the safest places in the County for a defence against the dark,' I told her. 'The boggart will probably be able to deal with most of what Loki sends against us. We can take care of the rest.'

'We can try,' Jenny said. 'But what if he attacks the village again?'

'In that case I'd have no choice but to go and help. But even if we travelled for miles and chose another location for the coming battle, he could still attack the village. I don't think he'll repeat himself in that way, though. He has the capacity to conceive of and create many tulpas – and a preference for new things rather than repetition and ritual. We have that in common. As a young monk I hated saying the same prayers over and over again. Endlessly doing the same things crushed my spirit. I'm of Loki's blood and I've probably inherited those traits from him. No, he won't attack the village. He'll do something different – something totally new! Something that pleases his love of novelty. He'll be bringing his own imagination to bear upon the problem of how to best destroy us.'

'Let's hope you're right,' Jenny said.

We reached the house and went upstairs to grab a few hours of sleep before breakfast. It was reassuring to know that the howl of the boggart would warn us of any attack. It was better to sleep whenever we could. The days and nights ahead of us promised to be exhausting.

I opened my eyes to see the sun streaming through the window. I must have been woken by the bell rung by the boggart. I dressed quickly. It wouldn't do to be late, and I was really hungry and looking forward to a big plate full of eggs, bacon and tomatoes.

Downstairs I passed the library and became aware that something was different. I came to a sudden halt. *What is it?* I concentrated until I realized what it was. The old grandfather clock was no longer ticking. I made a mental note to attend to it straight after breakfast.

Immediately as I walked into the kitchen, I knew that something – something so much more than a stopped clock – was terribly wrong. There was no fire in the grate, just cold ashes. There was no food on the table. It was bare without even a single plate or item of cutlery. There was no tantalizing smell of cooking and the room was distinctly chilly.

Jenny walked into the kitchen behind me. 'Where's breakfast?' she asked. 'Can't get the staff these days!'

The cheerful expression on her face faded as she met my eyes. I took my staff from where I had left it leaning near the door and led the way out into the garden.

A cold wind was blowing from the north. We walked between the leafless trees until we found the boggart.

It was dead.

10

MYRDDIN WYLIT

'Sorry it's cold. I can't face cooking, can you?' Jenny said.

I shook my head. We were back in the kitchen, sitting together at the table facing the plate of ham sandwiches that Jenny had made. We selected a sandwich each and began to nibble. I'd lost my appetite.

Pieces of the boggart had been scattered among the trees – fur, flesh and bones. Except for its head, which had been impaled on a stake driven into the ground.

Together we'd collected its remains and buried them in a grave among the trees. It was strange to think that Kratch would never guard the house and garden again, never howl a warning to intruders.

That was another strange thing. The boggart *hadn't* growled a warning of the attack. It had never screamed in rage. There had been no indication that a struggle was taking place. That suggested that it had been taken completely by surprise.

What kind of tulpa had Loki sent to destroy it? It must have been very formidable. Unless the god had done it himself . . . ? The boggart had fought battles against powerful opposition before – that was how it had suffered the first loss of an eye. It had driven off the Bane, a fallen god with great powers. Later it had lost the second eye but had still remained a terrible opponent. Nothing had ever breached its defences.

The form it showed to humans was that of a monstrous cat. But, of course, the boggart had been more than that. It had been a powerful spirit. Now that had been destroyed and all that remained was buried beneath the sodden earth.

'That boggart served spooks here for over one hundred and fifty years,' said Jenny. 'I can't believe that's come to an end.'

'It began with John Gregory who made a pact with it,' I said. 'In return for its services, it could devour any enemy that entered the garden. It was good that it made the breakfast but guarding the house was its most important role – now that is over.'

'So we should move on now. We're at risk every moment we stay here,' said Jenny, placing her half-eaten sandwich back on the plate.

I shook my head. 'Remember my wolves?' I asked.

Jenny nodded. 'What happened to them? They were gristles, weren't they?'

I nodded. 'Yes, they are gristles and nothing has happened to them. In summer I usually send them north into the colder lands that they're more suited to. But I think I'll summon them back to Chipenden. I think the cold weather in the County will be to their liking and we need them to fight alongside us.'

'How long before they can get here?' Jenny asked.

'I can contact them with my mind. When they get here depends how far north they've gone but hopefully they'll be back in two or three days.'

'That may be too long. We're sitting ducks here. Whatever killed the boggart could easily have slain us while we slept.'

'But it didn't. That suggests that Loki is still playing games.'

'Perhaps. But for how much longer?'

'Look, Jenny, I won't blame you if you leave but I'm staying here. This house has been a rock, a defence against the dark for centuries. Many generations of spooks have been based here with their apprentices and, live or die trying, each one did their best to fight the dark. It's my duty to remain. I refuse to run. I won't be driven out.'

'Wulf, I already told you, you don't get rid of me as easily as that. If you're staying, I'll stay too but I still believe we'd do better to keep moving – probably north to meet those wolves of yours a bit sooner.'

But, for now, we stayed. We took it in turn to patrol the garden and late in the afternoon walked together down into the village to stock up on provisions.

So it wasn't until late in the evening that I went into the library to get the grandfather clock going again.

I opened the double doors below the clock face and reached inside to set the pendulum swinging. But it was gone. It had been removed. I felt a chill like icy-cold fingers moving up and down my spine.

Someone or something had been in here to do that. Not only had it killed the boggart, it had come into the house.

For a moment I decided Jenny was right. We should flee north while we could and fight on the run. The house was no longer defended, and whoever this was could get into the house as they liked. But then I felt my resolve harden again. I would not be driven from the Chipenden house.

I went to Jenny and told her what I had found, giving her another chance to leave. As I expected, she refused.

Shaking my head at her stubbornness, I moved out to the edges of the garden and called, 'Seeds!' I planned to create a twisted thick border of ivy around the house. But nothing happened. There was no bitter taste in my mouth. No seeds appeared for me to spit out and use.

Pan's power must be reducing further all the time as Loki's grew – now his gift to me was of no value. Knowing it would be fruitless too, I tried once more to call for Thorne as it was now dusk. Again nothing happened.

Until the wolves arrived, Jenny and I were fighting alone.

That night we took it in turns to be on guard. I let Jenny have the first watch while I was supposed to return to my room and try to grab some sleep. But I didn't do that. I waited downstairs, watching Jenny through the windows whenever I could. I was unable to put from my mind the way the boggart had been taken by surprise and killed before it could even call out a warning.

I didn't want that happening to Jenny. I didn't want to wake up, go out to relieve her and find that she'd been slain.

When it was my turn to take over there were only a couple of hours or so before dawn, the hours of darkness short in this strangest of midsummers. I patrolled the garden for a while then faced away from the house, sitting with my back to a tree to wait for daylight.

I was finding it really difficult to keep awake despite shivering with cold. My eyes kept closing and the effort to keep them open was real.

Maybe I did nod off to sleep. Maybe I didn't. When I opened my eyes, I saw a tall, bearded man standing under the tree opposite me. He glared down at me.

As I said, he was tall – probably taller than the warrior, the shape I had taken while I kept watch. He wore a black cloak and a hood, which was pulled forward over his forehead. Despite that, the pale grey light enabled me to see his face. It was stern and that of a man of advanced years. His expression was filled with resolve, and something in the way he held himself suggested that he was strong and vigorous. He was carrying a staff and looked every inch a spook.

Then he spoke. 'Well, lad, no doubt you think that you're dreaming. Despite all you've achieved, you've still got a lot to learn. The first thing is to know the difference between waking and dreaming!'

I tried to clamber to my feet but found that I couldn't. My tulpa body wouldn't respond.

'Best you just sit still and listen to what I have to say,' he said, a faint smile on his face.

'Who are you?' I asked.

'Many called me Old Gregory, but not to my face. My name is John Gregory and I was the spook here for many years more than I care to remember. Time is short – so no more questions. Now, hearken to my words.'

Could this really be John Gregory? He didn't look like a ghost. There was no faint glow to him, and he looked as substantial as the tree that he was standing in front of.

'You need help,' he continued, 'and someone who can do that may be summoned. You met him in the dark – although he doesn't always dwell there – where's he's known as the Piper. But his true name is Myrddin Wylit. *You* can't call him down to earth though. He will only respond to one of the Samhadre. So you need the girl to do it. She's here with you, yes? Jenny. He'll respond to her because he's also one of that ancient race of beings.'

Then he was gone, simply vanishing. I came to my feet trying to rub the sleep from my eyes. How could that have really been John Gregory? Had it been merely a dream – one of the strange ones I sometimes got just as I awoke?

I went into the kitchen, found the frying pan and did my best to make breakfast. When it was nearly ready, I called up the stairs to wake Jenny and tell her that her food was waiting. We sat together at the table and started to eat.

'Sorry the bacon's a bit burnt,' I told her.

'It tastes good to me!' Jenny said with a grin. 'I like my bacon crispy.'

'I spoke to someone in the garden while I was on watch. I don't think that I was dreaming and he didn't look like a ghost. He said he was John Gregory . . .'

Jenny looked worried. 'It could have been a tulpa, Wulf!' she said. 'You told me how tulpas had replaced Tom and Alice and they looked and sounded really convincing. This could be just the same!'

'Well, Jenny, I don't have your ability to instantly know. But my instincts tell me that he wasn't one. I didn't get the chance to call him out because I was too busy listening to what he had to say. Then he vanished. But there's a way to put it to the test. When I was in the dark, Grimalkin introduced me to someone they called "the Piper". He helped us in our battle against the Fiend and his supporters. He was the one who gifted me the sword that I use when I'm in the shape of the warrior. John Gregory said – and for now let's assume that it *was* Spook Gregory – that we could call the Piper to earth to help us fight Loki. Or, to be accurate, *you* could summon him. That's because he's a Samhadre also. His true name is Myrddin Wylit, apparently.'

Jenny whistled through her teeth. 'He was the most powerful mage of all the Samhadre – born in the first age of our people when we fought against the demons of the dark and some of the Old Gods. If he came to earth, he could certainly help us here. But this could still be a trap – one of Loki's tricks!'

'Well, there's only one way to find out for sure. If you summon him and he arrives you'd know instantly whether it was or wasn't a tulpa.'

Jenny nodded.

'Then when shall we do it?' I asked.

'At dusk – that's the time when the windows to other worlds are open the widest. But we need water – a small lake would be best. If he answers my call, he'll emerge from the water.'

'Yes, that's what he did when I met him in the dark. He emerged from what they called the "Mud Lake". The best place I can think of locally is a small fell called Nicky Nook to the west, near a village called Scorton. There are a couple of small tarns there. And it's not too far away.'

We set off in plenty of time to arrive at the larger of the two tarns before dusk. Although the air was crisp and cold, the sky was a clear blue and the sun mildly warm on our faces as it slowly sank towards Morecambe Bay, where the sea sparkled in the far distance. As we walked, I asked Jenny a few questions about the Samhadre and her own lives.

'How many lives have you lived?'

'This is the third one. The first was short – I was attacked by a water witch while walking along a canal with Tom Ward. I hadn't been his apprentice for very long. In my second life I became his apprentice again, completed my training, worked as a spook in many different lands and lived almost to old age.'

'So, like Myrddin Wylit, some of the Samhadre are much older than you?'

'Oh yes!' said Jenny. 'Some of them have had hundreds of lives. We had an early civilization when humans were still dressed in animal skins. They were hunters and hadn't even begun to farm the land. As I told you, in the First Age of the Samhadre, my people fought some of the Old Gods and the demons that supported them. The war lasted hundreds of years and neither side could really claim victory. But it limited the power of the dark and resulted in a much safer and happier existence for humans who were then only starting to build their first villages and small towns. The Second Age included another war fought against powerful human witches and mages. By then we were in decline. We lost that war and were almost wiped out but once again the power of the dark was limited for a long time.'

'So this is the Third Age of your people?' I asked. I wondered if this age too would be one filled with war for them.

'I suppose it is,' said Jenny with a frown, 'but the only other Samhadre I've met was my own mother who explained what we were just before she died. I found some more material in a library in a desert land far to the east. But for all I know I could be the last of the Samhadre – but for this mage who must surely be dead, beyond re-birth, and living on another plane of existence. Maybe I'll ask him about that – that's if he arrives, or doesn't turn out to be a tulpa created by the Trickster God!'

We arrived at the tarn as the sun dipped below the horizon. I'd never been there before but it proved to be a pleasant spot with a few trees close to the water, the tarn being far larger than I expected. I'd studied the maps in the Chipenden house but such diagrams didn't always give you the full sense of what to expect. And it was far different from the Mud Lake in the dark. Here, the water was crystal clear and you could see right down into its depths.

By then it was becoming a lot colder and the clear sky suggested that tonight there would be a heavy frost. We waited a while for the light to begin to fail and then Jenny stepped to the very edge of the tarn.

She stared at the water and waited in silence for a minute or so. Then she called out the mage's name in a loud voice: *'Myrddin!'*

The response was immediate. A dark shape like a huge fish rose towards us. Then something pointed broke the surface.

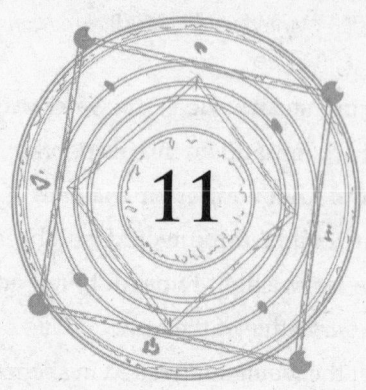

11

THE ONLY TRUE SAMHADRE ARE MALE

The Piper was exactly as I remembered from our first meeting in the dark. A tall pointy wide-brimmed hat burst from the lake followed by the long, bearded face which had green eyes with pupils like those of a goat.

The Piper wore his long green gown, with wide sleeves reaching to the tips of his fingers. As previously he seemed to be standing on the surface of the water, but this time his feet and the hem of his gown were visible although still immersed.

Water cascaded from his pointy hat although his gown appeared to be dry and this time it was not coated with green slime below the knees.

'What do you want of me, child?' he asked Jenny in a very bad-tempered voice. 'Why have you disturbed my sleep?'

'I'm sorry to disturb your sleep, Lord Myrddin,' Jenny said, bowing very low, her head almost touching her knees. 'Please forgive me. But we are in grave danger and I am here to beg you to help. We think it was John Gregory who directed us to your wisdom.'

I was shocked by the way that Jenny had spoken to him. He was a powerful being and deserving of respect, but she was almost grovelling before him – I'd never seen her speak like this before! But I had to make allowances because this was different for her. This was an ancient, powerful mage – like a king, and she was one of his subjects. I supposed she was behaving in exactly the way most likely to draw from him the response we desperately needed. She was doing what she had to do in order for us to receive his help.

'John Gregory . . . a stubborn spook if ever there was one,' the Piper reflected, turning his attention to me with a frown. 'And talking of . . . Here you are again, Wulf! There's always trouble when you're around.'

I wasn't going to be as obsequious as Jenny but I bowed politely, saying nothing, and let her continue the summary of what had happened, concluding with the death of the boggart and the theft of the grandfather clock's pendulum. Then she paused before adding the fact that I had sent for my wolf gristles but it could be a while before they arrived. And that we expected Loki to attack at any time – probably tonight.

The Piper shook his head sadly. 'There *is* a war in the dark, and for our side – the side against the god you mention – things are not going well. My strength is needed there, so any help I can provide on earth is very limited.'

'What happened to Pan?' I asked, speaking for the first time. 'Is there any way to bring summer back to the County? Soon people will begin to starve. I'd like to help them.'

'Pan is safe for now but his powers are limited as you have guessed. At the moment, I can say no more for who knows who may be listening?'

'And what about Grimalkin and Thorne?' I asked. 'Are they safe too?'

He shook his head and my heart fell into my boots.

'They have been slain?'

'No. They have vanished and I have searched for them without success. Whether or not they still exist, it is impossible to know. I can do nothing more for them, but I will try to help with your immediate problem. I will summon the nearest Samhadre and command them to help you to defend your home.'

'Are there any?' asked Jenny.

'There are, child. They are scattered to the winds, and the majority who still survive live in far distant lands. But there are some nearer – including a few here, within the County. Although their powers have waned, they are still formidable.

But now I must go – my strength is urgently needed elsewhere . . .'

Then he began to sink slowly into the water until even the tip of his pointy hat was submerged. We watched for a few moments as he descended into the depths, a dark shape gradually becoming smaller and smaller.

'A pity that he couldn't stay a bit longer,' said Jenny. 'There was so much that I wanted to ask him. But I'm happy to learn that I'm not the only one of the Samhadre left on earth. It'll be really good to meet some of my own people.'

We returned to the Chipenden house cautiously. As we climbed through the gap in the hedge, I remembered sadly how the boggart used to challenge me before moving away. I was struck again by the great loss.

As far as I could be sure there was nothing in the garden that could threaten us, but we could already hear small creatures moving through the long grass, small nocturnal animals such as hedgehogs and field mice, things that would not have got inside when the boggart guarded it.

The most dangerous part of our return was the actual entry to the house. I opened the door slowly and immediately heard a pattering in the distance. It sounded like mice. Previously, the house had never had such creatures scavenging within its walls. But now it was open to anything from outside. As I paused and listened intently, the house became absolutely silent, an oppressive stillness, as if something was holding its breath.

Together, we checked every room starting from the top floor. As we came down the last flight of stairs, I could hear a ticking in the distance. It seemed to be coming from the library and I already knew what it was.

We walked in to find that the grandfather clock was working again. Within the glass doors below the face of the clock, the pendulum could be seen swinging from side to side.

'I didn't hear it ticking when we came into the house,' said Jenny.

'Neither did I,' I replied. 'Maybe the pendulum had already been replaced while we were on our journey to Nicky Nook and just set going by dark magic while we were upstairs?'

Jenny shrugged. 'In either case somebody or something has been in the house again to replace it. Loki is threatening us. Showing us how he can come and go as he pleases.'

I smiled, trying to be reassuring though inside I was feeling anything but. 'What's done is done. I'm hungry so let's go down to the kitchen and grab something to eat before we make a plan.'

It was my turn to make the sandwiches and I filled them with cheese, tomatoes and pickles.

'A few more pickles on mine, please, Wulf!' Jenny said. 'I got the taste for them when I was last here. Alice used them a lot!'

That made me feel really sad. I remembered all those years ago how Alice and I had quarrelled as I stepped through the secret door in Hrothgar's house into the dark to fight the Fiend.

'*You don't scare me, witch!*' I'd cried.

I had been angry but I shouldn't have said that. After all, we had been friends and had worked together fighting the dark. And she had been Tilda's mother. They were words I could not take back. I could not ask her forgiveness. It was one of my big regrets. Things had changed so much. Alice, Tom and Tilda were dead, and the boggart had been destroyed. Maybe I would soon be joining them . . . I gave myself a shake. No matter how much you missed the past, you could never go back to the way things had been. I needed to be in this moment, for this war.

After we'd eaten, once again Jenny took the first watch while I paced up and down inside, taking careful glances at her through the ground-floor windows.

When I took over, Jenny went upstairs to bed. I changed into the boy, Wulf, as I thought it only proper that with my hood, cloak and staff I should patrol the garden of the Chipenden house as a spook. I was confident in assuming that less formidable shape than that of the warrior; I could change back in a second.

My confidence was a mistake.

They came just before dawn. Tall fierce gaunt men in dirty green cloaks, armed to the teeth.

No sooner had they emerged from the trees than I heard the door open behind me and Jenny ran to my side, gripping her staff.

'You should be in bed gathering your strength,' I told her. 'Have you been watching through the window?'

'Of course I have, Wulf! After all, it's what you usually do,' she said with a grin.

The tall men approached slowly. Their hair was long, unkempt and greasy. They halted a few feet short of us. Were these the Samhadre, whose help the Piper had promised? They looked hostile rather than friendly.

'Are they tulpas?' I asked Jenny, keeping my voice low. She shook her head then addressed them directly.

'Are you the Samhadre we were promised?' she asked as they came closer.

'Yes, and we're here to sort out your little problem, girl,' their leader said with a smirk.

'I'm Samhadre too,' Jenny told him, smiling politely. Then she grinned, her eyes sparkling. She was pleased to meet some of her own people for the first time. But her grin quickly faded.

'The only true Samhadre are male,' said the tall warrior contemptuously. 'You have our blood within you so that makes you fit to serve us. But nothing more. The best you can hope for is to become a wife.' He turned and smiled at one of the men behind him. 'Chutu, you are in need of a woman. She is yours, my friend!'

Then, to my astonishment, he seized Jenny by the hair, swung her around with great force and sent her staggering back towards the warrior called Chutu, while she desperately tried to keep her balance.

These warriors were supposed to be our allies.

To them, I was a boy far beneath their notice. Had I been in the shape of the warrior it would have been different. But I wasn't about to let their behaviour continue. Angrily, I drove my staff into the ground and went to help Jenny. I never got there. The leader backhanded me across the mouth hard and I fell to my knees.

'You'll keep out of men's business, boy – that's if you know what's good for you!' he snarled at me.

I came to my feet, spitting blood, in a rage and capable of anything.

In an instant I changed into the warrior. 'Sword!' I cried and heard the pleasing rasp as it dropped into the scabbard on my back.

I drew it and advanced. 'One at a time or the lot of you at once! It's all the same to me!'

'No, Wulf!' Jenny cried, her face twisted in pain as Chutu gripped her hair tighter.

The leader took a step backwards and held out his palm towards me as if to fend me off. But he wasn't looking at me – he was staring at the blade, which was burning with red fire, reflecting the light from the rising sun.

'Where did you get that weapon?' he asked. 'And who are you?'

'It was a gift from Lord Myrddin,' I told him. 'My name, as you probably realize, is Wulf. Now release Jenny.'

'I did not realize that she belonged to you,' he said with a shrug. He made a gesture and Chutu scowled but let go of Jenny's hair and she walked towards me.

'She belongs to nobody,' I told him. 'Once you understand that, we'll get along much better. I welcome your help. We expect the first attack at dusk.'

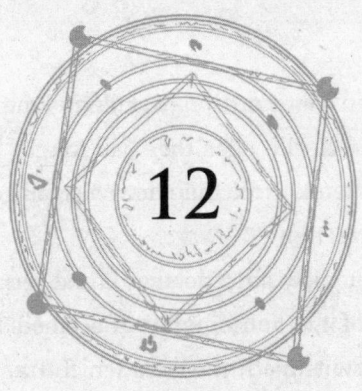

12

THE ARENA

As expected, at dusk they came: a horde of monstrous gristle tulpas in shapes that approximated human. Some had more than three arms and one head wasn't the norm. They bristled with weapons and came with clear intent to kill. It seemed that the Trickster God was no longer playing games. But there was no sign of him as the three-eyed demon – or in any other form that I could tell.

So what shall I say of that battle? Shall I describe how the ground was soaked in rot and slime as the tulpas were slain and disintegrated – that the slopes that led up to the house were heaped with the enemy dead?

This is all true; however, I will spare you the details.

We suffered one casualty – Chutu, who died bravely. I did not like the Samhadre. Having met the Piper, I had expected noble warriors but these were rough, uncouth and degenerate men – they must have fallen a long way from the First Age of the world when they had fought the Old Gods. Jenny would have to work out what she made of them in her own time.

Despite their surly attitude, they could certainly fight. At the low part of the battle, when it seemed that we must surely be overwhelmed, their leader, Korta, and I fought back to back.

Finally, such was the extreme threat of our own deaths that I took on the shape of the sky wolf. I let the wraith take over, almost totally surrendering my own human personality. And it unleashed a savagery that I had never experienced previously, even when fighting the Fiend in his winged demonic form. The slope that led up to the house became a killing ground – it was truly a slaughter on the hill.

And by dawn we had won, won another battle in this long war against the dark. The enemy fled or were unable to do so. I thanked the Samhadre and offered them breakfast. They declined, saying that they would make their own arrangements and stay nearby.

Jenny and I cleaned up as best we could and grabbed a few hours' sleep. I felt that with our allies camped close to the house there was no need to take turns keeping watch.

We walked out into the garden again early in the afternoon, to find a sheep being roasted on spits over a roaring fire. The Samhadre had chopped down one of the garden trees for fuel and I imagined Tom Ward's angry face at that outrage, but I made no comment and simply asked Korta where he'd got the sheep. He pointed towards the lower slopes of Parlick Pike, the nearest fell to the Chipenden house.

I knew who had owned the animal, so I visited the farmer, apologized and paid him handsomely for his loss. It was far more than he would have got at the local market and he was best pleased, inviting me to help myself and take from the flock whatever I needed.

Spooks are not generally well paid. At this rate my funds would soon run out but I had no choice but to feed our guests – saving our lives as they had. We offered them potatoes, carrots and onions to go with the mutton but they refused. They preferred to eat just the meat, slicing the carcass with their knives.

Later, we joined them round the fire to eat. The air was cooling and it was good to feel the heat on our faces. As we chatted, I noted that their attitude towards Jenny had changed dramatically and they talked to her with a new respect. After all, they had seen that she could fight as well as any man, and in the heat of the battle, with no thought of her own safety, she had intervened to save at least two of them.

She only picked at the tough greasy mutton, eating very little. What she was hungry for was knowledge of her people. They told her tales of heroic Samhadre exploits. But what she really wanted was knowledge of their situation now, how many of them there were, where they dwelt and how they lived their lives. They were not very forthcoming, and from what little was said I guessed that they lived in underworlds, in scattered groups distant from each other, above all safe from human eyes.

They took it in turns to tell her of the great battles of the First Age, beginning with the tale of Thurton, who had fought a demon lord, slicing him into pieces so fine that they had blown away upon the wind and it had rained blood for three days and three nights. No doubt at the core of each story was a fragment of history but they had been embellished into legends by repeated telling.

This went on until Jenny and I were the only ones still awake.

Feeling that Jenny was safe enough with the Samhadre, knowing that they would wake at the first warning of danger, I wandered off into the house carrying the dirty plates and cutlery that we had used for our mutton, potatoes and carrots. I washed them in the kitchen and as I came out into the corridor I noticed the silence.

The grandfather clock had stopped ticking once again.

I walked into the library and bent to open the glass door to send the pendulum oscillating again. The moon shone through the window and the glass was gleaming. Instantly, I saw the backwards writing. It was a magical message from a witch.

I bent closer to read it.

Wulf,

Return to the stone circle immediately!

Grimalkin

Grimalkin was alive! I was both delighted and astonished. Had it been her stopping and starting the clock to try and get my attention all along?

Then my heart sank a little as I was assailed by doubts, wary of more trickery.

I needed to travel back to the stone circle as soon as possible. I knew that I would have to take Jenny with me. After all, it might be another deceit by Loki and only Jenny could tell instantly whether I was confronting the real Grimalkin or another tulpa. Trickery or not, I would not risk leaving the real Grimalkin and Thorne trapped in that underworld.

Rushing back outside, I woke Jenny and told her about the message.

'It's better that the Samhadre stay here while we journey to the stone circle,' I told her. 'It's not just a case of defending the house . . .'

'You think he might take it out on the villagers to hurt you?'

'Yes,' I said. 'I do. Let's see if your people will stay to protect them.'

They didn't need much persuasion, and promised to patrol the outskirts of the village at frequent intervals. So, at dawn we set off on our journey northwards.

We walked fast. I was in the shape of the warrior and Jenny very much a spook carrying her staff with her hood pulled forward against the light drizzle that began as soon as we reached Cumbria. But although it was misty and wet, the leaves were still on the trees and the air warm as befitted the month of June. I worried again about how the County harvest would fail and its folk would face a winter of starvation.

By dusk we were back just north of Lake Windermere, and there we sheltered for the night in a barn, taking it in turns to keep watch. We slept for no more than two hours each then pressed on before the sun had cleared the horizon.

I pointed out the inn where I had first seen the witch and her familiar – both eventually proving themselves to be tulpas. I knew how fortunate I'd been to encounter Jenny. But for her, I could have died at the hands of the tulpa quisitor. Then, if I had somehow survived that, I would have fallen into the trap of the tulpa witch and her dog familiar.

By early evening we'd reached Keswick and walked on towards that small town. It was no good going directly to the stone circle as Grimalkin would not be able to contact us during the daylight hours. Apart from a small portion of crumbly cheese that we'd shared, we had pushed on without pausing to eat. Now both of us were ravenous and we found a tavern where we ate large slices of meat and potato pie with mushy peas. After that we wandered around the extensive market listening to the traders harangue the crowds who gathered before their stalls. Only as the light slowly began to fail did we start to climb the hill towards the Castlerigg stone circle.

Though as we passed his cottage we did not again encounter the man who had warned us before, everything else was exactly as I remembered it.

But for Jenny this was new and she gasped as the light of the moon strengthened by the minute, gleaming from the standing stones, and a mist began to swirl at our feet. Together we stepped into the circle and immediately the moon vanished and the sky glared with the baleful red of an underworld.

Now the stone house was clearly visible and we walked towards it, alert for danger.

'Wulf!'

The door was shut but Grimalkin called out to us before we reached it. Her voice seemed to come to us from an immense distance and had a slight echo to it.

'Is it you, Wulf? Why did it take you so long?'

123

'I came as quickly as I could.'

'You must have walked. Why did you not take on the shape of the sky wolf and fly here directly? Didn't you know that this was urgent? I bade you to come immediately.'

'I have Jenny with me and I could only travel at her fastest pace.'

'Jenny?'

'She is one of the Samhadre. In a previous life she was Tom Ward's apprentice.'

'She could have followed you while you came here directly. Why did you delay for her?'

'To verify exactly who you claim to be. One of her gifts is to know a creature to be a tulpa as soon as she comes close to it.' I turned towards Jenny. 'Is it Grimalkin or is it a tulpa?' I asked.

'I can't be sure,' Jenny said, shaking her head. 'I can't see her and she's far away. I need to be a lot closer. Why don't you call her out?'

I nodded. Why not?

'You are not Grimalkin. You are a tulpa!' I cried.

I heard laughter and it sounded like that of Grimalkin. But immediately I knew it was not. I sensed a powerful scary presence within those walls, hidden from our sight.

The laughter ceased and the creature that had sounded like Grimalkin spoke to me, the voice gradually deepening with each word.

'Well, it is time to put ourselves to the test, Wulf! My blood runs in your veins but it is much diluted because your parents were both human. It is hard to explain why you have such excellent ability as a tulpar. I have watched with astonishment the way you have developed your exceptional talent in only a few short years. Most tulpars, even over many human lifespans, have not reached your level of ability. Soon I will become the ruler of the dark – serve me and you will be well rewarded.'

Here we were. Loki had now called me to face him one on one.

I shook my head, but before I could put my refusal into words, Loki burst forward with a torrent of arguments as to why I should serve him.

'The dark lacks stability and has done so ever since the first fall of the Fiend,' he said. 'And strife within the dark has dangerous consequences for humans who walk the earth, oblivious to the fact that it leads to problems for humans – war, pestilence and famine to name just three. A strong ruler would bring stability.'

'What about the County?' I asked. 'Are you responsible for the early onset of winter there? And what of Pan?'

'Pan opposed me and so his power has been severely limited. As for your County, it is Golgoth who has brought the early winter.'

'You told him to do that!' I snapped angrily.

'And why not?' demanded Loki. 'After all, the greatest opposition to the dark has always come from your County. Your spooks have damaged us badly. Even your witch allies such as Grimalkin have inflicted severe hurt upon us. It is right now that the County suffers. It is well deserved. Perhaps in a few years I will relent.'

'In a few years it will be too late. Soon the people will start to die of hunger!'

'Then perhaps you can do something about that, Wulf . . .'

Suddenly a figure appeared before us. He was standing directly in front of the door, leaning back against it, completely at ease. A boy, carrying what appeared to be a guitar, and he was smiling at Jenny.

'You!' Jenny cried, raising her staff and taking a step towards him.

'Hold her back, Wulf!' the boy commanded. 'There is no need for her to die here.'

I put my hand on Jenny's shoulder and drew her back to my side. She put up no resistance but I could feel her body trembling with anger.

'I met Loki in my previous life,' she said angrily. 'He took this form of a boy minstrel and he deceived me. I thought he was my friend.'

'How easily you were fooled!' Loki boasted. 'Perhaps you would prefer me to take this shape!' The boy became the green-skinned three-eyed demon – the one who had escaped my trap back in Chipenden. 'I have a challenge for you, Wulf. A little contest. Let's test our skills against each other. If you win, I will bring summer back to the County. If you lose, you will give up your allegiance to Pan and serve me as I rule the dark. What do you say?'

He was the Trickster God. Would it be a fair contest? It wasn't in terms of how we were matched, anyway. How could I hope to beat a god who was the original source of my abilities as a tulpar? Yet to refuse the contest might lead to our immediate destruction. The ominous way he had said 'There is no need for her to die here' made me fear he might slay us both now where we stood. We were standing within an underworld that he controlled, after all. Who knew the true extent of his power here?

I remembered venturing into an underworld with Spook Johnson, one controlled by the goddess Circe. Witches cannot fly – that is a story believed by foolish people. But a witch had flown on a broomstick there. Almost anything was possible in an underworld.

This was a dangerous place to be. I regretted setting foot in the stone circle, entering yet another trap.

'What of Grimalkin and Thorne? Where are they? Do they still exist?' I asked.

'They do, but they are trapped in a labyrinth from which they will never escape. Unless I permit it, of course!'

'Then if I agree to your contest, in addition to the restoration of summer to the County, I wish you to free Grimalkin and Thorne and not to prevent them moving freely between this world and the dark.'

There was a pause, and then: 'I can agree to that but must warn you that if they use their freedom to move against me, they will be destroyed instantly.'

I nodded my acceptance and glanced at Jenny who was still scowling towards Loki.

We looked at each other with grim resolve.

'What form will the contest take?' I asked of the god.

Loki stepped back from the stone door and it opened with a grind. Within I could see rows of flickering candles. 'Step inside and I will *show* you and explain the rules.'

Both Jenny and I moved for the now-open door.

'No!' said Loki. 'You must enter alone. The girl would be wise to step outside the circle until this is over.'

'You can talk to me directly!' Jenny shouted furiously at the god. He paid her no mind and I moved to calm her.

'It's better if you do wait outside the circle, Jenny,' I told her. 'When this is over I'll walk out to meet you there.'

'Don't do it, Wulf,' Jenny pleaded suddenly. 'Please don't fight him alone – he'll destroy you.'

'You know that I've no choice. This is a chance to save the County and free Grimalkin and Thorne. I have to try. You'd do no less.'

Jenny nodded sadly then turned away and began to walk back towards the outer stones. When she reached them she simply vanished, to relative safety beyond the underworld.

'Now, follow me, Wulf,' Loki instructed, 'and I will show you what must be done. The rules are simple.'

Everything within the stone house had changed since my last visit, with Thorne. The inside betrayed common sense; it was far larger than the external dimensions would have allowed. But this was the underworld and the normal rules of geometry did not apply.

Beyond the small candle-lit hallway, a simple door now led into a vast cylindrical space constructed of large slabs of dark stone. Tom Ward had once told me about Malkin Tower, the Pendle home of the Malkin clan of witches. This seemed similar to what he'd described then. It was like being within a vast chimney, the roof so far above that it was lost in darkness. There were no windows. The floor crunched as I stepped upon it. It was gravel covered in sand.

'This is the arena where we will fight,' said Loki. My heart sank. 'There is a room for each of us, where we can prepare for combat. Follow me . . .' He led the way across the floor of the arena towards a couple of doors. 'This is yours.' He opened the door on the left.

I followed him through into a room obviously prepared for the creation of gristle tulpas. It was very similar to the one in which I'd worked when Hrothgar trained me. There was a long sturdy oaken table, upon the surface of which was just one item – a small knife. On the flagged floor, there were separate heaps of dust, ground bone and rotting vegetation and a small glass jar of what appeared to be blood.

'That's animal blood.' Loki pointed to the jar. 'But use your own if you prefer.'

I realized that was what the knife was for – to bleed myself and add it to the material from which a gristle would form.

'Now I will explain the rules . . .' he said with a malicious smile. He paced up and down the room before coming to a halt facing me. 'You may fight me alone in the form of any wraith that you have already created, or with a gristle ally that you may choose to create here. Are the rules clear?'

I nodded.

'One further thing. If you defeat me in the arena, if you slay me, it will not be permanent. I will be able to continue my existence in another wraith. Normally, Wulf, *you* cannot do that. If one of your wraith tulpas is slain, they are *all* slain and it would be the end of you. But here I will grant you a special dispensation. If you are slain, your wraiths will still cease to exist – they will be gone forever. But I will save your soul and place it within a wraith that I have already created for that very purpose. You will not like the tulpa in which I preserve your life but if you are diligent in my service then eventually I will provide something better! Do you understand?'

'Yes. How long do I have before we fight?'

'Take your time, Wulf. Time is nothing to me. When you are ready to fight you will find me waiting in the arena. Oh – I will fight alone in the shape I am in now. I do not need a gristle. Do not be fooled into thinking that I fled fearfully from the valley where we fought near Chipenden. I did it to avoid destroying you. I thought you were interesting – as you have my blood in your veins, I wished to amuse myself and study you further.' And with that he left for his own room.

What kind of a gristle would have a chance of defeating Loki? It made good sense that I should create one, because surely two of us would have a better chance of victory than one? What worried and disturbed me was Loki's extreme confidence – his certainty that he would win and without any help from a gristle.

I would use the warrior wraith to fight. After all, he was strong and fast – very difficult to beat. But I had never seen that three-eyed demon fight. What weapons would he use, what combat skills did he have?

It had been my custom when being trained by Hrothgar to jot my ideas for a new tulpa down on paper – then choose the best of my selection and create it. But there was no pen and paper here. I just had to use my imagination, hold my ideas in my memory and come up with something that would complement the warrior's abilities. I had already created six wolf tulpas which even now were travelling south to join me. Should I create a seventh? It could harass and distract Loki while the warrior moved in for the kill. That would at least give me a slender chance of victory.

I didn't like the blade left for me on the long table, the invitation to use my own blood. That technique had always reminded me of the way a witch dealt with a familiar – often feeding it her own blood. I didn't like that similarity to evil practices from the dark. When I'd created the wolf gristles, it had been Tilda who had used her blood to give them life.

Perhaps I would be better off without a gristle ally but I couldn't deny that I would need all the help that I could get. Things were looking grim.

13

A FIGHT TO THE DEATH

I took a deep breath and strode into the arena to find Loki already there waiting for me. He was gripping two swords of a type that I had never fought against before, but I knew they were scimitars; each had a thin sharp curved blade.

'So, you fight alone, Wulf!' His three eyes glinted at me in amusement.

'I prefer it this way.'

I was not totally without confidence. The warrior had never lost a battle – so far.

We moved towards the centre of the arena.

'Begin when you are ready, Wulf. The first move is yours.'

I drew the sword from the scabbard on my back, gripping it in my left hand. I attacked immediately. Feinting, by striking towards Loki's head before flicking the weapon from my left hand to my right and slicing horizontally at his throat, I almost won with that first attack.

But the god was lithe and very fast and he stepped back quickly so that I fell short of my target. He grinned, then remarkably the two blades that he gripped began to spin. His wrists were rotating like wheels, those scimitars whirling faster and faster. He raised his long arms high above his head and they bent back impossibly. His green-scaled arms were triple jointed.

Somehow, I managed to block both blades but then, before I could recover, he attacked. This time I only managed to deflect one blade. I twisted away, but the second struck home close to my shoulder blade though thankfully not penetrating my mail. We faced each other and he grinned at me – an expression that said that I had no chance against him and he could finish me off any time he chose. Well, that may be, but I was going to go fighting hard.

I retreated under the pressure of his second attack. The fight very much belonged to Loki and it was taking all my skill and ability simply to defend myself. The warrior was unaccustomed to such combat. Usually, this wraith always attacked and rarely had to fight defensively.

With his spinning wrists and triple-jointed arms, the Trickster God was beating me and soon I could see that he'd had enough of this fight which hardly challenged his abilities.

'I am disappointed, Wulf! I expected more from you than a clumsy desperate defence. You are beginning to bore me!' He laughed and slid the blades of the scimitars together as if sharpening them. 'So let me tell you about the wraith I've chosen for you to see out your days . . . Soon you'll find your soul inhabiting a creature that you would never have chosen – a pig!'

I grimaced and re-gathered my own blade.

'It was one of the goddess Circe's first choices of a creature to transform her enemies into,' Loki continued. 'I liked Circe and served her for a while, just as I once served the Fiend. But, all the while, I was biding my time awaiting the chance to become what is my destiny – the ruler of the dark. You played a part in destroying Circe. And then Grimalkin and Thorne finished her off. How fitting it will be to hold you in that shape as long as it pleases me, while Grimalkin and Thorne wander that labyrinth for all time. And long before that the people of the County will have died in a long cold winter that will never end!'

He advanced towards me and my thoughts scrambled desperately for some way that I might defeat him. Then it came to me. The sword! It had strong magical power and had been loaned to me by the Piper. Which would be the stronger – this powerful sword or the two scimitars created by a god? There was only one way to find out . . .

He attacked, obviously determined to finish me off this time. The scimitar in his right hand wounded me high upon my left arm. I felt it cut through the mail and slice into my flesh. But I ignored the pain. It was the scimitar in his left hand that I was interested in. As it cut down towards me, I brought the sword upwards with every atom of my strength.

The two blades clashed with a metallic sound.

But it was *my* blade that shattered!

I stared in dismay at the stump of the sword. All that remained was the hilt and about five inches of jagged blade. Desperately, I hurled myself at Loki. For a few seconds my fury and speed drove him backwards. But he recovered almost immediately, his counter strikes swift and clinical.

I felt the blows strike home. I felt his blades penetrate my mail, cutting me to the bone. I fell to my knees, dropping the stump of the blade from my nerveless hands. Blood was running into my eyes and blinding me, running in rivulets from my wounded body to splash upon the floor.

'It is done, Wulf,' Loki said as he stood over me. 'There is no need for you to suffer any more pain. I will end you now and then you can begin the next stage of your existence.'

Before I could react, he brought the two blades down hard and fast. It was over quickly with surprisingly little pain. I felt my life end. There was darkness and then, in my very last moments of awareness, a terrible knowledge.

14

THE TRICKSTER

As Loki slew the gristle identical to my warrior form, I attacked.

In his arrogance and delight in displaying his fighting skills, the demon god had not noticed me hovering high above his head close to the ceiling. He had been careless. I was in the shape of the sky wolf but had made myself very small – no larger than a mote of dust.

And I had kept exactly to the rules he had laid down. I had constructed a gristle to fight alongside me – one in the shape of the warrior whom I had given my own memories and sense of self. Against my better judgement and feelings of distaste, I had used my own blood to give it life.

My gristle had fought well but hadn't really had a chance against Loki. It wasn't holding the real sword loaned to me by the Piper so the weapon had shattered on contact with the magical scimitar wielded by a god. I only hoped that my gristle had not realized its own true nature before it died – that would have been terrible for it.

So now it was my turn. The real me. Growing rapidly as I swooped towards my target, I took Loki completely by surprise, ripping the sight from his left eye, flying clear of his blades before he could react. I soared right to the high ceiling, pulled my dark wings close to my body and stooped to my prey, dropping as fast as a stone.

Blood now running down his face, half-blinded and taken by surprise, he struck upwards desperately but both scimitars missed. In this form I was much larger than he was and I gripped both his arms above the elbow, my talons piercing the flesh to the bone. The swords dropped from his hands as I carried him aloft before swinging his lower body again and again like a pendulum against the curved stone wall of the arena.

Then I dropped him and he fell hard onto the flags below. He had just managed to clamber up onto his knees again before my final attack. Without a moment's more thought, I ripped and tore him, driving the life from the wraith that housed his being.

I landed and changed back into the form of the warrior. The wraith that the god had inhabited was dead, lying in a pool of his own blood. Not far from him, on the flags was the disintegrating body of my gristle, now little more than a heap of slime and a few tattered rags of clothing.

I had won!

For a moment I allowed myself to feel triumphant, pushing aside the true knowledge that the god was not *truly* destroyed. He would have fled back to the body of another of his wraiths as he told me he would. He might be watching me even now. Would he keep to the rules, fulfil his part of the bargain? Accept his defeat? I had tricked the Trickster but I had kept to the rules. Would he do the same?

In answer to my fears, a third door opened in the stone wall and Grimalkin – the actual assassin this time – and Thorne walked out onto the floor of the arena. They looked down in astonishment at the dead wraith and what remained of my gristle.

'Wulf! What has happened here?' Grimalkin looked confused.

The wraith was not made of earthly things like rotting leaves and there was no slime. It simply began to disappear, the large third eye in the centre of its forehead the last fragment to vanish. Thorne shuddered at the sight.

'I'll explain once we're clear of the circle,' I told them in response to their immediate questions. 'It could be dangerous to remain here for too long.'

We walked together from the stone house and beyond the circle of stones where immediately the baleful red sky of the underworld gave way to pale stars, an increasing brightness to the east warning that dawn was not very far away.

Jenny was waiting there. 'Wulf,' she cried. 'I thought that I'd never see you again! It's been a week since I came out here.' And she pulled me into a hug.

I noticed Thorne's face tighten in dismay as we embraced. I assumed she was jealous of my friendship with Jenny but this was no time to comment on it. Instead, I gave an account of everything that had happened and how I had defeated Loki. Then I explained what I had won by my victory.

'Summer will return to the County, and you two,' I said, smiling at Grimalkin and Thorne, 'are free to pass between this world and the dark as you wish. But take care because he threatened that if you act against him in any way, you will be destroyed. That was his warning.'

'Thank you, Wulf. Once again, I am grateful to you.' Grimalkin gave an evil smile showing her pointy teeth. 'It is almost dawn and we will leave for the dark immediately. But don't worry about us. What we need to do is find the crossroads and seize the cauldron. Then we can return to earth exactly where we choose. And it has its own power – which we can use against Loki. I heed his warning but will not obey his wishes!'

She looked like she was ready to leave immediately. 'One last thing,' I said. 'It was John Gregory who directed me to the Piper for help. He came to me in a sort of dream.'

Thorne looked disbelieving but Grimalkin was not. 'Old Gregory would always want to help a fellow spook when he could – even in death.'

And never one for pleasantries, without saying anything else, she gestured to Thorne and they took their usual transit form of silver spheres which floated up into the sky and were lost from sight as they journeyed back to the dark.

Jenny and I walked south at a brisk pace and by noon were approaching the Cumbrian lakes. We called into a tavern and had lunch together while I gave her a more detailed account of the battle with Loki and how I had won.

'But what will he do next?' asked Jenny. 'Surely that's not the end of it?'

'We'll just have to wait and see,' I replied. 'Grimalkin and Thorne are free and I expect Loki to have kept his word and allowed Pan to return summer to the County. So there's nothing more I can do but carry on dealing with the dark as a spook whenever and wherever I meet it in the County. There have been three rulers of the dark in the past century or so – the Fiend, Circe and now Loki. We'll have to learn to live with the most recent one as he regains his strength.'

We finished our meal without speaking of it again, instead talking about what we'd do when we returned to Chipenden. Jenny was keen to return to her conversations with her fellow Samhadre.

What we had was a temporary truce with Loki, but at some point it would be broken. No doubt that would happen if Grimalkin and Thorne succeeded in winning possession of the cauldron again.

When we crossed the border from Cumbria into the County, the summer weather remained the same. The leafless trees were already beginning to bud and no doubt the farmers would be desperately ploughing and sowing again, hoping that there would be sufficient time to have a late harvest. So far, so good.

We reached the Chipenden house early in the evening to learn that the Samhadre had gone the previous night. They'd left us a note and it seemed that they had been called away on urgent business. To my surprise, they left us coins as well – full payment for another two sheep which they had seized, slaughtered and devoured.

Jenny was disappointed at their leaving. 'I suddenly felt less alone for the first time in my life, Wulf,' she told me. I understood this feeling.

Then there was a howling in the air and I grinned at her. My grey wolves were back! They had waited here patiently for me to return. We had new guardians for the house and garden. I had called them back when the land had suffered under the onslaught of winter weather, but knew they would stay with me now the summer had returned, even though the warmth was not to their taste.

Soon I was on my knees patting them while they greeted me enthusiastically, their tongues lolling from their mouths while a wary Jenny kept her distance.

'Do they have names?' she asked.

'Of course they do!' I introduced them one by one: Tooth, Claw, Blood, Bone, Hide and Hair. 'They're named after the wolf hounds that a spook called Bill Arkwright once used to hunt water witches across the marshes,' I explained. 'And, of course, there's a seventh but that's one of my wraiths. I call it Black Fang but I won't show it to you now or the others will get over-excited!'

'Good idea. They look excited enough already!' Jenny exclaimed.

'Maybe I will, actually!' I said, grinning and changing my mind. 'As it's warm, let's eat outside tonight. I'll go hunting with the wolves for our dinner – they'll enjoy that – and I'll bring back food enough for two!'

Jenny looked at me doubtfully but I had already changed into Black Fang and, after one quick backward glance at her startled face, I led the barking wolves away at speed through the Chipenden garden and up onto the lower slopes of the Bowland fells. They fed well upon rabbits and hares but it was a struggle to keep them away from the sheep. In my wolf shape, I was full of bloodlust and eager to eat my prey raw, but my human self prevailed and I delivered a couple of large rabbits back to the garden less than two hours later.

'You did the hunting, so I'll do the cooking!' grinned Jenny. 'But you can skin them for me first.'

I did just that, then I watched Jenny cook them to perfection using two spits over the flames while I buried potatoes in the hot ashes at the edge of the fire.

Soon we were dining, the wolves out in the trees guarding the boundaries of the garden, and it was only as we finished our meal that I asked the question that had been on my lips for some time.

'What will you do now?' I asked.

She smiled at me, her face lit faintly by the stars overhead. 'I think I'll stick around a bit if you don't object – in case there are any unpleasant surprises from Loki. Then, if all seems settled, I'll be on my way. I can track the Samhadre and I intend to follow them back to their refuge and learn as much as I can. So, until then I'll help you with the local spook's business. But not as your apprentice – as your partner!' Jenny grinned.

'That sounds good to me.' I had known that I couldn't keep her at Chipenden for long. I would miss her, but Jenny had her own life to lead.

So it was that we dealt with the local spook's business that had accumulated in our absence. In truth, there wasn't that much of it – a couple of hauntings, a malevolent witch who ended up in a pit in the garden and a boggart that was persuaded to move on.

Twice during this time, Grimalkin left a message using the mirror by my bedroom. She and Thorne were still searching but had not yet found the cauldron.

All around us the farmers were busy with their sowing, and the conditions were now perfect for it. No sooner was that done than weeks of showers came, perfect for germinating seeds. No doubt Pan was controlling the weather, carefully creating optimum conditions. I should thank him at the right point. I suspected that the summer would be followed by an extended autumn and there would be more than enough time to reap the harvest.

Then at last came the day when Jenny was ready to leave.

'Thank you for all you have done,' I said sincerely. 'I hope your people will give you the answers you seek about your lives.' And I hoped they'd be more welcoming to her than they'd been when they first arrived at Chipenden – but I kept that thought to myself.

'I've been proud to fight at your side, Wulf. And to put my old spook skills to practice once again. If you'll have me I'd love to return later in the year.'

I told her I'd be very happy with that and we hugged goodbye.

I'd been sad at the farewell but returned to routine tasks, taking my mind off it – until one day I was summoned at the withy trees crossroads to deal with something different and more dangerous.

15

WITCH DELL

Dealing with an undead witch was never easy.

Some of the Pendle witches were content to let their dead go smoothly to the dark. But others had a family tradition of taking the newly deceased witch and burying her in a shallow grave in Witch Dell to the east of Pendle Hill.

When the next full moon shone down upon the grave, the witch would then become undead and scratch her way to the surface. Most of them were weak, barely able to scrabble around in the mud beneath the trees, existing upon a meagre diet that was mostly composed of worms and slugs. But a few were very strong and ranged far from the dell, hunting down living human prey. In the end it came down to the same thing. Bit by bit the undead witches decomposed and rotted, losing limbs and other parts of their bodies. Then they went to the dark.

It was a family tradition, and caused a lot of problems for spooks. When the bell at the crossroads rang, it was a young lad sent by his father to tell me that a newly undead witch was wandering all over the Pendle district and killing farm animals. I knew that it was only a matter of time before she turned her attention to human prey.

It was my duty to deal with it, so I left immediately, arriving at Witch Dell after dark when I knew that the undead would be stirring.

I was in the form of the warrior. I knew that my mail armour, which came down to my wrists and ankles, should partly protect me from the fangs and talons, but I was still wary of a sudden attack. I moved cautiously into the trees, listening carefully. At first, I could only hear the sighing of the wind and the creaking of the branches. Soon there were other disturbing sounds – the rustling of dead leaves agitated by the wind and the slithering of what could have been a snake but was far more likely to be crawling witches.

I took another few steps, taking me deeper into the trees. I came to a halt and listened carefully again. I could hear nothing but I felt something that sent shivers up and down my spine.

Something was stroking my boot. Before I could react, it changed into a fierce grip. In one swift movement, I drew the sword from the scabbard on my back and swung it down in an arc, cutting through the wrist of the undead witch.

She gave a gasp and I heard her begin to crawl away through the mounds of leaves.

I moved deeper into the dell, even more vigilant now. I remembered what Tom had once told me about Witch Dell. It was where Malkin witches fought each other for the prize of becoming the next witch assassin. Grimalkin had triumphed over her rival even though the other witch had created traps – deep hidden pits, at the bottom of which were sharpened stakes waiting to impale Grimalkin. Those pits were still here in the dell. I had to be very careful not to fall into one.

Then I heard running, the rapid slap of bare feet on mud and grass. A tall witch passed by, not more than twenty paces in front of me, and ran to the edge of the dell and out onto the bare hillside. This had to be the one! At any one time there was rarely more than one undead witch with the strength and power to do this. So I followed her.

For a few minutes I ran behind her, the distance between us gradually closing. Then I changed into the sky wolf tulpa and soared into the sky. It took me mere seconds to swoop down, grip her shoulders and carry her away. She fought crazily, spitting and shrieking, struggling to tear herself free of my grip. She had no fear that if she succeeded in twisting out of my grip she would fall hundreds of feet onto the hillside.

The feel of her body was not pleasant and the sky wolf did not like this burden of rotting soft and squishy flesh. But it held her firmly and flew far beyond Pendle Hill and then over the waters of Morecambe Bay.

There I released her, watching as the undead witch fell into the sea where the salt water would quickly destroy her. Then I swooped lower and allowed my talons and feet to trail through the water to wash away the stink of decay.

Spook's business completed, I soared aloft again, gained altitude and headed back in the direction of Chipenden.

Passing over a wood far below I saw a strange glow among the trees and felt an insistent tug inside me, making me want to see what it was. Curious, I swooped lower.

As I did, I caught an eerie haunting sound. Realizing what it was, I landed.

It was the pipes of Pan.

I changed into the form of the boy, Wulf, dressed in the garb of a spook and carrying a staff, and followed the sound.

Pan sat in a clearing in the trees surrounded by his creatures. He was in the shape of the benign pale-faced, fair-haired boy – not the terrible adult shape that caused panic and terror in all who beheld him. Sitting cross-legged on the ground playing a reed pipe, creating the eldritch music that had compelled me to his presence, his face was reassuringly human but for the pointy ears protruding through his long unkempt hair, and the long green toenails of his bare feet, each one curling upwards into a spiral.

Around Pan was a dense crowd of creatures, and although it was the middle of the night and many of them were nocturnal, all were charmed by the music of his pipes, gazing upon him with adoring eyes. Badgers, voles, mice, foxes, rabbits, snakes and shrews, they all were intently watching him play. Overhead the branches were bowed with the weight of birds, totally silent, mesmerized by his music.

Pan ceased playing and placed his pipes on the grass before him. He smiled at me and gestured that I should sit down facing him. I bowed slightly to show my respect.

'You are welcome here, Wulf. You have just done me a great service so that I am once again free to come and go as I wish – as long as I do not move against Loki. Or at least not so that anybody notices!' he said with a grin. 'Your victory was achieved with imagination and bravery, I hear. Perhaps we should rest now? What do you think? Or should we continue with our war against Loki?'

'It's not for me to say,' I said. 'You know far better than I do the balance of power in the dark. What more could we do? And what would our chances of victory be?'

'Well, I have been thinking about that. We cannot attack Loki directly but there are ways in which we could significantly weaken his power further. As you know, each god who becomes the ruler of the dark needs allies. Those allies support them, doubling or sometimes tripling their power. There is one significant ally of Loki that we could attack . . .'

'You mean Golgoth?'

'Yes. I would like you to slay the Lord of Winter for me, Wulf.'

That was easier said than done. Golgoth had killed the formidable Grimalkin and hurled her spirit into the dark. But I was still in Pan's debt – and perhaps, truth be told, I was beginning to find only doing spook's business a little tedious.

'If you wish it, I will try,' I told Pan.

'Have confidence, Wulf. I have not regained my full former strength or Loki would not have been able to limit and bind me so easily. But you, Wulf, are a different matter. Through skill and ingenuity you defeated Loki and before that you destroyed the Fiend. I believe you will be able to deal with Golgoth! Let us end this war!'

I opened my mouth to reply but could think of nothing that would change his mind, which was clearly made up.

'There are two ways in which you can reach Golgoth. There is a burial mound up on Anglezarke Moor to which he may be summoned. It might be possible to take him by surprise. But my preferred option is to go to a mage – one of a race of people called the Kobalos. They dwell far to the north and once fought a war against humans. The one you should contact goes by the name of Slither and he knows another, better way to reach Golgoth. I will contact Grimalkin and she will tell you where he may be found. Once she and Slither were enemies but are now allies.'

'Grimalkin is well and still searching for the cauldron,' I told him – although I suspected he already knew this.

'She is, Wulf,' he confirmed. 'But she is also becoming more confident that she will soon locate and seize the cauldron. Of course, once she achieves that it will bring her to the notice of Loki and his allies. So, all the more reason that we destroy Golgoth first. Time is of the essence.'

16

THE STORM

As I flew back towards Chipenden I felt apprehensive about what Pan had asked me to do.

It was one thing to stand against the dark and slay its denizens in the County and beyond. It was far more dangerous to venture into Golgoth's lair unprovoked. I suspected that he would have created an underworld close to our world. It would be a dangerous and unpredictable place. And as for the dark itself, I certainly didn't want to venture there again either. Even if I survived, I might return to find that many years had passed on earth. And the last time that had happened, I had lost so much.

Back at the house I went straight to bed and slept. I was exhausted and didn't wake until many hours after dawn.

After frying my own breakfast of mushrooms, bacon and eggs and once more lamenting the death of the boggart – the wolves were doing an excellent job as guards but not as cooks! – I went into the library to do some research and discover what dangers I faced in confronting Golgoth. The first book that I consulted was *The Spook's Bestiary*, a catalogue of creatures from the dark, written by John Gregory. I briefly wished the old spook would appear again and share some more of his wisdom in person. But, still, at least I had his written words . . .

One extract made me feel that I had no chance at all against such a powerful Old God:

He has the power to create pockets of cold so extreme that human flesh and bone become brittle and can shatter into fragments.

I also learned that Morgan, an apprentice of Gregory's who had gone to the dark, had tried to raise Golgoth but died at the hands of the god, shattered into fragments – just as the passage indicated.

Even more terrifying was the death of Grimalkin. This was written up in one of Tom Ward's notebooks and told how they had ventured into the burial mound and raised Golgoth, hoping to slay him the moment that he materialized. But they had failed to take him by surprise. Brave beyond any hope of success, Grimalkin had attacked him, but – like Morgan – he had frozen her, and when she fell her flesh and bones had shattered into fragments of ice, hurling her spirit into the dark. Only then at the pleading of Alice had Pan attacked and defeated him.

I wondered at the many attempts of those before me: human against god. Would it be foolish to confront Golgoth up on Anglezarke Moor? It would perhaps be better, as Pan had suggested, to await what Grimalkin had to say and hope that this mage called Slither could provide me with a better way to approach and slay the god.

Like most of the Old Gods and powerful demons, Golgoth could not walk the earth unless summoned by a coven formed of many united witches' covens. But now I had to go and confront him in his own domain where he would be all-powerful. I needed every bit of help I could get.

I searched the library, looking for anything at all that I could find about the Kobalos and its mages, such as this Slither. Most of it was in the form of entries in Tom Ward's notebooks and I had to do a lot of reading to find them. Then I discovered something else in the library that promised to be very helpful indeed:

An Extract from the Notebooks of Nicholas Browne, a Spook from Ancient Times: GLOSSARY OF THE KOBALOS WORLD

Anchiette: A burrowing mammal found in northern forests on the edge of the snow-line. The Kobalos consider them a delicacy eaten raw. There is little meat on the creature but the leg bones are chewed and digested also.

Askana: It is the dwelling place of the Kobalos gods. Probably just another term for the dark.

Baelic: The ordinary low tongue of the Kobalos people used only in informal situations between family or to project friendship. The true language of the Kobalos is Losta, which is also spoken by humans who border their territory. For a stranger to speak to another Kobalos in Baelic implies warmth and friendship but it is sometimes used before a 'trade' is made.

Balkai: The first and most powerful of the three Kobalos High Mages who formed the Triumvirate after the slaying of the king and now rule Valkarky.

I realized that some of these entries were no longer valid. The original Triumvirate were already dead, slain during and soon after the war with humans. It made me wonder how the political situation in Valkarky might have changed since that war was over. Was the new Triumvirate less belligerent and more friendly towards humans?

I read on . . .

Berserkers: These are Kobalos warriors sworn to die in battle.

Boskka: This is the breath of a Kobalos mage which can be used to induce sudden unconsciousness, paralysis or terror within a human victim. The mage varies the effects of boskka by adjusting the chemical composition of his breath. It is also sometimes used to change the mood of animals.

Bindos: Bindos is the Kobalos law that demands each citizen sell at least one purra in the slave markets every forty years. Failure to do so makes the perpetrator of the crime an outcast shunned by his fellows.

Bychon: This is the Kobalos name for the spirit known in the County as a boggart.

Chaal: A substance used by a Haizda mage to control the responses of his human victim.

Cumular Mountains: A high mountain range that marks the northwestern boundary of the Southern Peninsula.

Dendar Mountains: The high mountain range about seventy leagues west of Valkarky. In its foothills is the large important kulad known as Karpotha. More slaves are bought and sold here than in all the other fortresses put together.

Dexturai: Kobalos changelings which are born of human females. Such creatures, although totally human in appearance, are easily susceptible to the will of any Kobalos. They are extremely strong and hardy and have the ability to become great warriors.

Eblis: This is the foremost of the Shaiksa, the Kobalos Brotherhood of Assassins. He slew the last king of Valkarky using a magical lance called the 'Kangadon'. It is believed that he is over two thousand years old and it is certain that he has never been bested in combat. The Brotherhood refer to him by two other designations: 'He-Who-Cannot-Be-Defeated' and 'He-Who-Can-Never-Die'.

Erestaba: The Plain of Erestaba lies just north of the Shannah River within.

There was much more but I stopped reading and carried the book away from the library to study later at my leisure. Each entry was short but did provide a very useful summary of the Kobalos world I needed to learn.

It was almost a week before the message from Grimalkin reached me, and during that time I busied myself with local spook's business and reading as much as I could about the Kobalos.

There was a mirror on the landing outside my bedroom. As I walked by, on my way down to breakfast, it suddenly gleamed with a bright light then clouded. I knew that wherever Grimalkin was she had breathed upon the mirror and now would begin to write upon it. Sure enough, the words began to appear, the writing backwards as it always appeared to the recipient of such a message.

Wulf,

Cross the Northern Sea flying directly eastwards and then fly inland before heading northeast. When the land is covered in ice and snow watch for the confluence of two large rivers. At their junction you will see a huge tree set back from the edge of a forest. It is known as a ghanbala tree and is the home of the Haizda mage, known as Slither. I will warn him to expect you as he does not take kindly to being approached by strangers.

Grimalkin

I thought I should be able to find it – especially if I flew high enough.

I knew that Slither was a Kobalos, so why had Grimalkin called him a *Haizda* mage? The books I had read did not explain that fully. Neither did they explain the powers wielded by other types of Kobalos mage. Another thing bothered me too. The Kobalos lived in a frozen country of ice and snow. Surely they would *worship* a god such as Golgoth who created such conditions? They would certainly not wish to help me to destroy him. I had no idea what my visit to this creature would be like. I did not have time to do all the research I could have done into him and his people . . .

But I knew that Pan would soon get impatient and so, bidding farewell to the wolves who I left guarding the house, I wasted no time and, taking on the form of the sky wolf, flew east far beyond the County, reaching the Northern Sea before noon. There I rested and gathered my strength overnight hunting fresh meat, gorging myself so that I would have the strength to make the crossing. I had no idea what the extent of the water that I must cross was. The maps in the library did not extend their coverage that far.

At dawn I took to the air and flew directly east. I didn't like the look of the red sky, recalling that ancient saying: 'Red at night, shepherds' delight. Red in the morning, shepherds' warning.' Bad weather was on its way.

I flew on, noting the dark clouds forming on the horizon and the huge 'white horses' cresting the enormous waves below. The wind was blowing directly towards me, slowing my progress. I was trapped between two malevolent elemental beasts. And quickly, they struck.

The storm hit me like the blow from an irascible giant, attempting to force me down into the turbulent water which was eager to swallow and drown me. So I increased my size and beat my wings vigorously to attain a safer altitude. Increased size meant that I would use up my store of energy more rapidly but I couldn't afford to be small lest I be driven hither and thither like a leaf at the mercy of the elements.

I battled on for hours, flying into the fierce storm of wind and rain, the sea an ever-present threat below waiting to drown me. I had several wraith tulpas that I could use, but not one of them was at home in water. How I wished now that I had created something that could swim in the sea. But it was no use wasting time on such regrets. I had to fly on, hoping that my strength would see me to the safety of the distant eastern shore.

But how far away was it? I had no knowledge of the width of water that I had to cross. I had fought Old Gods and survived. Over the Fiend I had even triumphed. But their power was nothing compared to these elemental forces that cared nothing for me. Did Pan know of my plight right now? If so, why did he not intervene? After all, the God of Nature could control the climate and even volcanic eruptions of fiery magma that surged up from the depths of the world to burn and ravage its surface. And I was here on his business. Hopefully he would do what he could to protect me.

My mother had a favourite saying and it was she who had sent me to become a monk in Kersal Abbey all that time ago. She thought such a holy place would put an end to the terrifying nightmares from which I'd been suffering. She used to say: 'Heaven helps those who help themselves!'

17

ENTER AS MY BOUND PRISONER

My situation was growing more perilous by the moment. But as I looked down at the raging sea I was suddenly filled with new hope. Far below me was a ship, three-masted with tattered sails, dwarfed by the gigantic waves that rose above it. That could be my saviour right now.

Once directly above the ship, I adjusted my size and dropped through the turbulent air like a stone, unfurling my wings at the very last moment, correcting my position and alighting on the spar right at the top of the main mast.

I was not alone. By now I was no larger than a seagull and had to jostle for position among many of these birds. They seemed to have no alarm at my strange appearance and were no doubt more focused upon their own survival than being concerned about the strange, small winged wolf that had alighted among them.

Some birds preferred to continue flying rather than take the rest and refuge offered by the ship. I saw a stormy petrel fly east, overtaking us, and then something else, flying at the same speed as the ship. It was very high and kept being obscured by clouds, but, judging by its height and apparent size, I guessed it to be an albatross. Then a frightening thought struck me. What if it was Loki, the Trickster God, watching my every move? Had he worked out Pan's next move – and therefore mine? If so, there was nothing that I could do about it but I was relieved that, when the clouds cleared a little, the huge bird had vanished.

The ship rolled and shuddered each time a mountainous wave broke over its decks. I looked down at each one as the ship sank out of sight before bobbing up like a cork. Each time I wondered if the vessel would survive. But for one man, there was no sign of the crew who must be below battened down against the storm. There was a chair lashed to the deck and the man was tied to it, grasping the ship's wheel with both hands. He kept adjusting course so that we turned into every large wave to meet it head on. I supposed that was to lower the risk of the ship capsizing. Was this helmsman the captain?

I noted that we were sailing east into the teeth of the storm and I was being carried ever nearer to my destination. So that was good although our progress was slow.

At last, the force of the wind began to lessen and the sky began to brighten to the east. The waves had not decreased in size but no doubt that would take longer than the calming of the air. I waited an hour or so in case conditions worsened then I flew aloft again, disturbing the seagulls, and increased my size again, soon leaving the ship far behind.

In less than half an hour I could see the eastern shore. It was green and thickly forested and I alighted among the trees and now took on the form of the Black Fang tulpa. It was dusk so I hunted and gorged myself, building back up reserves of strength I knew that I would need to draw upon.

After that, what else was there to do but sleep? There was no fixed time for meeting Slither and I certainly wasn't going to rush into a battle with Golgoth. Once I had learned all that I could about him I would probably need to create at least one new wraith.

At dawn I took to the sky again and flew inland, then turned to the northeast as Grimalkin had instructed. On the third day of my journey overland, the landscape below me began to change. There were far fewer signs of cultivation, and the deciduous trees gradually gave way to an evergreen pine forest.

By dusk I was gazing down upon patches of ice below and the air grew steadily colder. Once again I fed, then rested.

But with the new day came a blizzard. I awoke to dense snow, and once aloft I could see very little below so again I changed into Black Fang and hunted for food. Even in the depths of winter, the County rarely produced weather such as this. I had once ranged far to the north with my grey tulpa wolves and we had hunted as a pack. How they would have loved it here! Still I silently thanked them for what they were doing back in Chipenden. I hoped I'd see them again.

It was afternoon before the weather cleared – and what a change! The air was still extremely cold but the wind had dropped to a light breeze and a weak sun shone down out of an azure sky. I flew northeast again, taking advantage of the pleasant flying conditions and the clear visibility.

Then suddenly there it was – the confluence of two wide rivers and a single strange tree standing close to the point where they joined, set back some distance from the edge of the evergreen forest exactly as Grimalkin had outlined. This had to be the ghanbala tree that was Slither's home. And it was very strange indeed.

It was not as high as I'd expected but it was incredibly broad; the diameter of the trunk had to be fifty feet at least. And it was strangely twisted, its long branches creating a dense canopy of broad leathery leaves.

I alighted about sixty paces from it and changed my shape to that of the warrior, walking slowly towards it, my boots crunching on the frozen snow.

I halted before the tree and heard a noise above me – a strange rasping. Small pieces of brown bark were falling onto the surface of the snow just in front of me but when I gazed upwards the foliage was too thick for me to see anything. Was it some type of bird feeding upon the tree?

Then something dropped through the foliage to land on two legs facing me. I looked at the creature in astonishment. Its face was very hairy with a snout, but like a human it was dressed in a long black overcoat that came down almost to the feet of its black boots. There were thirteen buttons, which looked like they were crafted from bone. To my astonishment, I realized he had a long tail that rose higher than his head and twitched alarmingly. The creature was exactly my height and gazed into my face with an impudent grin.

'You must be Wulf!'

As it spoke, its long tongue emerged from its mouth like a snake. 'I am Slither. I have been expecting you. May I congratulate you on an excellent demonstration of shapeshifting. I have rarely seen better. I watched you approach through the sky and guessed that it was you. Do you use tulpas?'

I nodded. 'Yes, I am a tulpar as well as a spook – that's my craft.'

'I am a Haizda mage and have magic of my own. Unfortunately, I do not shape-shift but like you I can change my size!'

Suddenly he shrank until he was hardly larger than a rat. He grinned up at me then became much larger again in a blink. He was now twice my size and grinning down. Slither towered over me and it took all my courage not to take a nervous step backwards. Then, once more, he was my exact size.

'Welcome to my home,' he said. 'Note that it stands proudly in a space of its own close to the two rivers. The River Shannah is slightly longer and wider,' he said, gesturing to the one behind us that flowed from east to west. 'It marks the traditional boundary between the Kobalos domain and the human kingdoms. The other river is called the Merca and in truth it is a tributary although almost as wide. Other trees cannot grow close to my ghanbala or they die, and I use my magic so that it retains its foliage the whole year round. It is also a gum tree and the sap that oozes from it has many useful magical properties. So now come inside and we will drink and dine together.'

I stared at the tree in puzzlement. Inside?

Slither grinned again, as if he had read my thoughts, then he pointed up towards the foliage. 'Most creatures who enter my home are dead and in pieces ready to be eaten, and I carry them inside through a cleft high in the tree. But for you it will be different!' he cried, his long tongue lolling from his mouth.

With a flourish he produced a huge bronze key from the pocket of his long overcoat, inserted it into some hidden lock within the bark and twisted.

You would never have guessed that there was a door, but the tree opened wide. I could see within and followed Slither into the ghanbala tree.

I had expected beds of leaves and grass and a rough-hewn table, but I was astonished to find plush, ornate furnishings. There were long leather couches and a large oblong table of polished oak upon which stood a thirteen-branched candelabra. Deep dishes of hot food steamed on the table on plates of the finest engraved pottery.

'You knew that I would arrive now?' I asked.

'Of course,' he replied. 'As I said I have powerful magic of my own. Those who underestimate me do so at their peril! Be seated and eat your fill,' Slither invited, and immediately started to heap his own plate with appetizing thick slices of meat. 'I am an omnivore!' he said with a wicked grin. 'I can dine on warm blood or cold radish. Variety is the spice of fine dining – do you not agree?'

I nodded as I started to heap food on my own plate. 'When I shift my shape I feed according to the needs and desires of the tulpa that I inhabit. So yes, in that respect we are alike.'

'It is good common ground – a place to begin. I wonder what else we have in common?'

'Grimalkin, of course. It was she who sent me to you – well, on the recommendation of the god Pan,' I told Slither. 'She thinks you could aid me in destroying Golgoth, but I would like to know why you would do this, when it seems to me he should be a god that you would support. After all, he produces the climate that suits your race.'

Slither gave me another of his feral smiles and allowed his long tongue to protrude from his mouth. 'We have many gods but it is certainly true that some powerful citizens within our city of Valkarky do think like that. It is ruled by a triumvirate of mages, and the original mages were more extreme in their views. Their support for Golgoth and one other god called Talkus was very strong. He was destroyed. To tell you the truth, I would be happy to see the same done to Golgoth. After all, once he ceases to exist Pan will provide for our needs.'

As soon as Slither began to fill his long mouth with food, I did the same. For a while we were silent, concentrating on eating our fill. Then Slither spoke again. 'Tom Ward slew the last of the three of the former Triumvirate. How is he? Grimalkin told me that you were once his apprentice.'

'He is dead now – peacefully, I think, of old age,' I told Slither sadly.

'Of course – humans are not as long-lived as we Kobalos. A new triumvirate, the successors of those who fought a war against humans well over a century ago, now rule our people. They are less belligerent, and there has mostly been peace between human and Kobalos since the war. However, they worship Golgoth as one of their chief gods, and I do not. You see I am what is called a Haizda mage and we have far different views than those who dwell within the city itself.'

'Is there just one city?' I asked.

'Indeed there is, but Valkarky is very large and there are Kobalos who believe that it will never stop growing until it covers the whole world.'

'That sounds impossible! How can they believe that?' I asked.

'I agree that it is very unlikely. They think that Golgoth will expand the freezing conditions there until that climate covers everything. Then we would be dominant and the building would continue unchecked.'

'What do Haizda mages believe in and why do they live beyond the confines of the city?' I asked.

Slither shrugged. 'We have always been outsiders with our own magic and philosophy that differs from those who dwell within Valkarky. So it is only natural for us to live beyond the jurisdiction of that city.'

I waited in silence for Slither to say more but he started eating again. I felt that there were things that he didn't want to tell me.

'Grimalkin said that you know the way into Golgoth's underworld. Is it far from here?'

'It is about a week on foot. Unfortunately, unlike you, Wulf, I am unable to fly. The portal to his underworld is actually within the walls of Valkarky and there lies a problem – there is no way that I could get you into that city undetected.'

'I have other shapes that I could use – one is a harmless mongrel dog . . .'

Slither shook his head. 'Whatever shape you adopt the gatekeeper will see you for exactly what you are. Its name is Kashilowa and there is only one reason for it to admit you into Valkarky – you must enter as my bound prisoner.'

'Is there really no other way?' I asked, unable to hide my dismay from Slither. 'Some way to bypass the scrutiny of the gatekeeper?'

He shook his head. 'I am afraid not, Wulf. Kashilowa is not a member of the Kobalos race. We make many creatures to help fight our battles and defend our city, and the gatekeeper is one of the most formidable. The creature is very large with one thousand legs and multiple eyes. It sees everything. And even if it could somehow be evaded, the Kobalos warriors within the city would take exception to the presence of an unbound human. All humans within Valkarky are slaves and must be seen to be so.'

I nodded grimly in resignation. 'How will I be bound?'

Slither gave a sly smile.

THE GATEKEEPER

'A chain will be put around your neck and it will be tethered to my belt,' Slither said. 'Do you not trust me, Wulf? I have welcomed you into my home. And you will not really be my prisoner. It would be easy for you to change your shape in an instant and cast off the chain.'

'It is Loki, the Trickster God, that I don't trust,' I explained to Slither. 'Recently I had a very bad experience. I was captured by some of his servants and my arms were bound. I wasn't worried in the least as I thought to break free at a suitable time. But when I tried, I couldn't do it. Loki had used his magic on the cuffs and I could not break free. I was trapped and couldn't shift my shape.'

Slither paused and stared at his empty plate. 'You defeated the Trickster God in combat – so Grimalkin tells me. He will leave you alone for now unless you act against him. Of course, attacking Golgoth may be considered to be the same thing. But you have done nothing yet. If he knows that you seek to enter Valkarky he may have suspicions but any intervention from Loki will come later – I am sure of it. Come, finish your meal and tomorrow, after you have slept and regained your strength after your long journey, we will consider the details of our enterprise.'

Without Jenny Calder at my side, for all that I knew the Slither I was talking to might have been replaced by a tulpa. I thought that unlikely but didn't bother to call him out – after all, he wasn't human and that might not work anyway. So I ate well and resolved to make the best of things.

The bed provided by Slither was very comfortable and I slept a long dreamless sleep, awaking completely refreshed. I wandered through the rooms within the tree calling his name but there was no sign of Slither. However, he had left me a generous breakfast and I enjoyed it gratefully.

No sooner had I finished it than I heard a noise outside.

The door opened and there was the mage wearing his long black cloak with its thirteen bone-buttons. At his hip he now had a weapon, a long sharp sabre. Over his shoulder I could see a large black stallion. Attached to the saddle were bags and also a very small round shield.

He grinned and nodded back towards the horse. 'I have borrowed this fine beast from a local farmer friend of mine,' he said. 'If necessary, it is strong enough to carry us both.'

'I've a shape that might prove useful for travelling over snow,' I replied.

Slither nodded. 'We can discuss how to deal with Golgoth when we make camp tonight. But first I need breakfast! I am glad to see you have already partaken.'

I waited politely while he ate his own fill and then asked a question: a question about my name, which I gladly answered.

'My name is Wulf. It's a shortened form of my full name *Beowulf*. It was suggested to me by Tom Ward. I think it's a suitable name because I can take on the shape of the sky wolf and also a savage wolf called Black Fang. So what about your name – does Slither have any special meaning?'

'It is the name I chose for myself when I came of age. That is what we Haizda mages do. When we become adults we choose the name that best describes our behaviour and inclinations. It is the sound I make when I swing with my tail from a high branch of my ghanbala tree before dropping to the ground to hunt down my prey. It is also the sound I make when I slither through a slit in a wall or floor to gain access to a locked, secret or private place. It is also the sound and sensation that an enemy feels and hears when I creep into his brain.' He grinned.

'You can creep into someone's brain?' I asked, filled with alarm.

'Fear not, Little Wulf, I will not slither into your brain! After all, you are my guest and my ally!'

I nodded and smiled but inside was filled with alarm at the thought.

After Slither had eaten, we set off due north. He was riding the stallion and I had become Black Fang whose fur matched that of the horse perfectly. Sometimes I raced ahead, delighting in the power of my body, at other times I loped alongside Slither and his mount.

The sky was clear and the sun shone down out of a blue sky but there was little warmth radiating from it. The snow was quite deep but frozen hard. It seemed that with every hour that passed on our journey north, it became colder.

As dusk approached, we made camp and I went hunting while Slither built and lit an enormous fire. I brought back plenty of meat and I transformed back into the warrior and we cooked it together before eating.

'Have you other *human* shapes?' Slither asked, licking his hairy fingers after eating his fill. 'It is simply that you will attract too many interested eyes if I take you into Valkarky in that splendid form. They will want to know where I encountered you and how I defeated you.'

I smiled and changed from the warrior to the boy spook complete with dark gown, the hood pulled forward.

'That is better,' he said. 'This is how we will enter.'

I slept well, taking on the shape of Black Fang who did not feel the cold and was content to sleep on a bed of snow. Slither didn't even bother with a blanket although I knew he had at least two in his saddle bags. Under that long black coat, I suspected that his fur was thicker than that of my wolf wraith.

We continued to travel and developed a routine each day. We discussed my attempt to destroy Golgoth but were no nearer to coming up with a plan that might work, so put it off for further consideration until we were within Valkarky. It seemed that Slither had his own private secure dwelling there and I would have a better idea of what lay ahead.

Then just before noon on the fourth day of our journey we encountered trouble. There was a band of mounted Kobalos warriors ahead and Slither considered them to be a threat.

'Hide yourself, Wulf. I will deal with them,' he said. 'Don't try to help. Not all of them will die here and I do not want them carrying back stories of our alliance to the city.'

The black fur of the wolf would be easy to spot, even from a distance – I had created it as a creature suited to the County, not a frozen land such as this with its white gleaming snow. So I became a very small sky wolf and soared aloft to watch what was about to happen.

Slither waited for the warriors to advance towards him. I noted that each wore a sabre at their belt similar to Slither's, but three of them also had long black lances.

They surrounded the mage and almost immediately voices were raised in a language I had never heard before. I might not have been able to understand the words but I could tell they were all spoken in anger and suddenly the warriors wheeled away from Slither before re-forming, the three with lances in their vanguard.

One of them lowered his lance to a horizontal position and charged directly at Slither. He looked certain to be impaled but, at the very last moment, he lifted the small round shield and used it to deflect the point of the weapon. It was astonishing that Slither could position such a small shield so accurately. And then his own sabre flashed in an arc, reflecting the red of the sun.

Another redness splashed upwards then – blood. The Kobalos warrior dropped his lance, fell heavily from his mount and sprawled in the snow. Wasting no time, Slither attacked a second warrior, another lance-bearer, and he met the same fate, his blood staining the snow red.

He chose the third lancer for his next victim and I was impressed by his combat skills. He was like the warrior, having great lethal economy of movement.

After the three lancers lay dead upon the snow, the remainder of the Kobalos fled, snatching up the reins of the loose horses as they left. Once they had disappeared from view, I flew down and took on the shape of the boy, Wulf.

'Will they bring more warriors and try to hunt you down?' I asked him.

Slither shook his head. 'The ones who carried the lances led the raiding party. They were elite warriors. Without them the others will simply return to Valkarky and report what has happened. But we must move on now – they will come back for their dead.'

'Why did they attack you?' I asked. 'Are Haizda mages considered to be enemies?'

'We are not very welcome in Valkarky, no, but tolerated. These idiots attacked because they wanted my stallion.'

'It's a magnificent beast – no doubt it would increase the status of its rider.'

Slither laughed. 'They wanted to kill and eat it. A black stallion is considered a great delicacy in the city.'

On the morning of the eighth day of our journey, I caught my first glimpse of the city of Valkarky. It looked like a long white cliff on the horizon.

'It looks huge,' I said. 'Is it built from ice?'

'No, it is not made from ice. I will explain when we draw nearer. We should reach Valkarky at dusk. But now it is time to fit the chain round your neck. Those who guard the city have sharp eyes – especially the gatekeeper! – and soon they will spy our approach.'

So I turned into the form of the boy spook and Slither fitted the black chain round my neck, tethering it to his saddle. I did not like it but had to accept the situation. How else was I going to enter Valkarky?

'How is it that the Kobalos have human slaves?' I asked. 'I thought Kobalos and humans had put the war behind them and now lived in peace?' Yet I remembered what I had read: under the law of Bindos, each Kobalos citizen had to regularly sell a slave in the market.

Slither grinned. 'It is true that there are no more large battles, Wulf, but the human principalities and kingdoms to the south are as warlike as my people and there are always skirmishes. The Kobalos also raid cattle owned by humans. During such fights prisoners are taken.'

It was beginning to grow dark as we approached but there were bright colourful lights on the northern horizon, a shimmering curtain containing the whole spectrum of a rainbow. It seemed to be coming from the walls of the city.

'What's the source of those strange lights?' I asked Slither.

'You also asked earlier what the city is made from and now I will answer both questions. The lights are beamed from the eyes and mouths of the creatures who are constructing Valkarky and expanding its size. They are called the "whoskor" and are not naturally born but are the products of Kobalos magic. They generate soft stone within their bodies then spit it from their mouths before crafting it into the required shape. After a few moments it becomes extremely hard.'

I had not read about this in my research before setting out, and as we got closer I could see the whoskor at work upon the walls. The eyes of these strange entities swayed upon long black stalks and their brown fur rippled in the breeze as they scuttled hither and thither working upon their task. The walls were uneven in height, clearly in various states of construction.

Slither urged his stallion to go faster and the chain tightened about my neck so that I staggered, almost falling. No doubt he did that to further convince any watchers that I was indeed his prisoner. I calmed my temper, reminding myself that this was simply for show – and that Slither had given me no reason to doubt his intentions.

We followed a narrow road that led up to a high metal gate, flanked on either side by half-constructed walls. The gate opened to receive us although there was no evidence of guards. We passed through several gates in a succession of inner defensive walls. These inner ones were already wide open, but, with a metallic clang, each slammed closed behind us, cutting off any possibility of retreat.

There were narrow windows above, no wider than arrow slits in a castle wall, and I wondered if we were being watched. Finally, we came to the largest gate of all which was closed against us. It was almost dark now but I could see well enough to note the tremendous height of the new wall that we faced. It towered up, lost to sight among the clouds. Although built from soft stone the walls hung with stalactites.

Two mounted Kobalos warriors, lances held vertically, waited on either side of the huge gate.

But my eyes were drawn towards a huge creature which now slid its way towards us, its long, pulsing body bristling with spines and its breath billowing into the cold air in great clouds. At first it was hidden by the thick white mist of snow kicked up by its multitude of legs, but this slowly settled and it was fully revealed to us.

It was a terrifying sight and I knew that this must be Kashilowa, the gatekeeper of Valkarky.

The gatekeeper suddenly scuttled forward and touched Slither's forehead with the tip of the long tongue that spiralled from its red mouth, which was so large that it could have swallowed Slither and his stallion in one mouthful. Whether this was some ritual greeting or a method of communication, I did not know. Was Kashilowa learning something about Slither by tasting him? Something about me?

Suddenly the gatekeeper roared out what sounded like a word while directing its multiple eyes in my direction. Its voice was a thunderclap that caused scores of ice stalactites to break free and fall from the wall above the gate.

Even chained as I was, I tensed, ready to fight at a moment's notice.

Slither began to shout back in a loud voice – in the Kobalos language, I assumed. I didn't know what he was saying but there was clearly anger in his words. Soon the gatekeeper was shouting back but twice as loud, causing more stalactites to fall and shatter. Already, things did not seem to be going well.

It gestured to me aggressively.

19

THE SKLUTCH

Then, very suddenly, the dispute seemed to be over. The gatekeeper turned away and climbed the high wall behind it, quickly disappearing from view. The two Kobalos lancers lowered their weapons and the gate opened to admit us. I glanced at Slither but he – still pretending I was his prisoner – didn't so much as breathe in my direction.

Slither gave what appeared to be a contemptuous jerk of the chain and rode towards the gate, dragging me behind him. Once through the gate the air was significantly warmer – rather than the freezing cold of our approach to the city, it now felt like a mild late autumn day back in the County. There were occasional glimpses of a darkening grey sky above us, but I saw that the city had a roof, and no doubt that accounted for the change in temperature.

We travelled through narrow streets of dwellings whose external appearance didn't differ too much from small human cottages. Once we passed a market with stalls although there were few customers and nobody gave us a second glance. At last, we reached Slither's second home, which seemed no different from the rest.

He left the black stallion outside and, still leading me by the chain, opened the door and tugged me inside. The first room we entered had a table and three chairs, tiles on the floor and torches on the walls which flared to life the moment that Slither glanced at them. Although it was far from luxurious, I was astonished by the cleanliness of everything. There was not one speck of dust in sight. Did Slither have servants who came in to clean when he was absent?

Slither was carrying my staff and he leaned it against the wall.

'Be seated!' he commanded. I bristled – behind doors I wasn't too keen on remaining his prisoner. But he speedily removed the chain from my neck, tucking it into the pocket of his coat.

'The gatekeeper didn't seem too welcoming,' I said as I took a seat.

'The foolish creature disputed my right to enter the city,' Slither replied. 'Many here do not like Haizda mages and think we should spend our whole lives as far away as possible. But it is more of a ritual than a real attempt to bar entry to Valkarky. It is my right to be here and I soon put the foolish creature in its place. Now rest and I will go and get us some food. Whatever you do, stay inside. Without my presence holding you chained, you would be slain on sight!'

I knew that I could venture out without drawing attention to myself. 'In the shape of the sky wolf I can make myself no larger than an insect,' I told him.

'You might get away with that but there is a risk,' he replied. 'Some mages have the ability to detect intruders no matter what form they take. Besides, it will be useful for you to be seen about the city as my property as you will discover later.'

Then, without further explanation, Slither went out, leaving me alone in his little house.

I was tired and despite my best efforts to stay awake, soon my eyelids began to close and I felt myself falling into a deep sleep.

I was awoken suddenly by disturbing noises. I could hear a clicking and a very loud rasping sound behind me.

I lurched to my feet and glanced at the wall. Attached to it was what appeared to be a large human head covered with long hair. Six multi-jointed legs sprouted from the place where one would have expected its ears to be. A huge oval mouth took up most of its face, leaving no room for a nose, and from it protruded three long tongues covered with backward-facing barbs. It seemed to be licking the walls, making a harsh rhythmical rasping sound as it did so.

Quickly I changed into the warrior tulpa.

'Sword!' I cried, and there was a different type of rasp as the weapon entered the scabbard upon my back. I drew the sword and advanced upon the hideous monstrosity.

The door opened suddenly and Slither stepped into the room, carrying food in a large woven basket. 'Put away your sword, Little Wulf!' he cried. 'This is one of my trusted and beloved servants and is no danger to you at all. Fungal growth and the accumulation of dust is a chronic problem because I am absent for long periods. Before you is just a harmless sklutch, one of the lesser servants that I employ. It is simply cleaning the walls with its tongues and sucking up the fragments that it loosens. But if you prefer it to be absent while we eat, I will send the creature away!'

Slither clapped his hands loudly. The ugly sklutch stopped rasping immediately and it scuttled down the wall and squeezed into a narrow crevice near the floor.

I returned my sword to its scabbard. In many ways I wished I had more time to get to know the ways and customs of the Kobalos. But I was keen to get on with the large and dangerous task that awaited us.

We sat at the table and Slither produced two bowls which he filled from the contents of his basket. 'Eat up!' he invited. 'I prefer meat as bloody as possible but this is a tasty alternative. It is cold food but delicious – a selection of the many types of fungi that are farmed within the city.'

I picked at the food a little uncertainly but it indeed proved to be delicious, each type of fungus having a distinctive sharp flavour. And it was very filling, a surprisingly good meal.

'So, as you prefer it, why aren't we having meat?' I asked. 'Is it hard to come by?'

'Not at all, Little Wulf, but very often it is not fresh and some of batches may contain the flesh of humans slain in skirmishes. There are many cults in the city, some of which prefer fungi to meat, so this is an acceptable alternative – I hope that you agree?'

I most certainly did!

When I awoke the next day, Slither was in the living room holding the chain.

'I am going to show you the location of the portal to Golgoth's underworld so that we may continue with our aims. But you will need to be tethered with this again as we must pass through many busy public thoroughfares.'

I made no complaint and bowed my head so that Slither could fasten the chain round my neck.

Then, holding the length of chain in his left hand, he gave a small tug, grinned and pointed towards the door. There was an expression of cruelty on his face. Did he enjoy leading me about the city in this way? Gradually, I was learning to trust him – but I wasn't enjoying being in this position.

And so he showed me the city. Valkarky was vast but very gloomy as we always seemed to be underground. Even the large open spaces that the corridors gave access to seemed like vast caverns, but their walls were perfectly smooth and clearly manufactured from the soft stone spat from the mouths of the whoskor.

We passed through a vast market full of stalls containing food. I could see no sign of the delicious fungi that we had dined on the previous night; instead, Kobalos were buying open metal bowls some of which contained small creatures that were alive. Worm-like entities squirmed as the purchasers greedily stuffed them into their mouths.

We moved on to pass through a succession of gloomy corridors mostly lit by flickering torches. However, in some areas the walls themselves seemed to radiate a white light. Kobalos that we passed mostly ignored us, walking by and gazing straight ahead as though we were beneath their notice. But when the rare curious glance came our way, Slither would give a sharp tug on the chain, jerking my head forward sharply. On one such occasion an involuntary cry escaped my lips and tears came into my eyes. I knew we were playing our parts but I had to wrestle down my urge to retaliate – it would ruin everything.

At one point on our journey we passed large steaming vats which were full of blood. 'Most warriors prefer blood to fungi,' Slither whispered, so nobody could see him talk to me. Each large vat was surrounded by a horde of jostling Kobalos warriors competing to dip their metal bowls into the blood, which they then slurped greedily so that much of it was wasted and dribbled down their faces and armour to splatter on the floor.

What was the source of the blood? I wondered. Valkarky was an extremely ugly place and I could not bear the thought of it expanding to cover even one more inch of the world.

There were other creatures at large in addition to the Kobalos. Mostly they resembled insects, ranging in size from that of a small dog to a bull.

Some scuttled by on many legs, as if on urgent business, while others loitered, twitching and active in the same location, maybe cleaning like the spider-like creature in Slither's quarters or engaged in some mysterious activity. No doubt they were harmless but their appearance made them seem threatening.

At one stage on our journey, we passed through a cavern full of huge moths, their wingspan wider than my hand. At first glance they had a certain beauty as their huge wings seemed to radiate a pulsing white light. But their bodies were like fat grey slugs covered with bristle and I was astonished when Slither caught one, tore off its wings and popped it into his mouth.

'They are somewhat chewy and a little gritty but they are delicious, Little Wulf. Try one. You will never forget the taste.'

I shook my head and we moved on.

At last, we reached our destination. Ahead of us was a large doorway, an arch in a wall of stone. It was guarded by four Kobalos warriors.

'Within there is what you seek – the portal to Golgoth's underworld.'

I was surprised. 'I expected it to be hidden away somewhere,' I told Slither.

'Why hide it away? Beyond that door is the Temple of the Lord of Winter. His priests guard the portal but you will not need to fight your way inside. Tomorrow I will give you to the priests as a sacrifice to Golgoth. They will push you through the portal. What happens then nobody knows. No living sacrifice ever returns. But now we will go back to my quarters so that you may eat, rest and prepare yourself for your ordeal.'

We turned and retraced our steps. I suppose that I had somehow expected that Slither might aid me in my attempt to destroy the Old God but it seemed not. But I couldn't complain. He'd done what was promised – shown me the portal and devised a way to get me inside.

Then I would be on my own.

20

I WAS THE PREY

Our meal was a further assortment of fungi again which were delicious but, as it turned out, the ideas that he fed me were even more nutritious. I'd been wrong – the mage *was* giving me more help.

'I cannot enter the portal with you because, if discovered, my existence henceforth would be one of hiding and desperate defence as Golgoth's servant-priests hunted me down. They would never give up,' Slither announced as if he had guessed at my disappointment that I must face Golgoth alone. 'Now I must ask you something – what tulpas do you own that you can inhabit and what resources do you need to create another?'

'I have seven tulpa wraiths that I can inhabit,' I explained, describing their special functions and abilities. 'There is another type of tulpa called a gristle that is a separate creature and to create that I would need blood, bone, leaves and other organic material – plus time and freedom from distractions. To create a wraith all I need is my imagination and the ability to bring great concentration to bear.'

'That is good,' Slither said. 'I say this to you because only after you have entered the underworld and seen Golgoth will you be able to decide what tulpa shape is best able to defeat and destroy him. I cannot give you any useful information because I have none.'

'What does Golgoth do with the prisoners that are given to him as sacrifices?' I asked.

Slither shrugged. 'I repeat – none ever return so we don't know. Maybe Golgoth accepts the tributes although he has no real need of them – gods sometimes do that because it is the faith of those who worship them that is vital to their continued existence. Maybe he has servants within his underworld that devour each sacrifice. We simply do not know. But I have hope that you will succeed, Little Wulf. For although you do not enter his domain with the power to destroy him, your ability to shift your shape gives you an excellent chance of evading his clutches for a while. And while you are free, there is hope – a possibility that you will devise a way to do what must be done.'

'Slither, I thank you for all the help you've given me but aren't you concerned that if I succeed or partly damage

Golgoth they will link that to your surrender of me as a sacrifice?'

'It is a chance that I must take, Wulf. The priests may well quickly deduce my guilt, but Pan has asked for my help as he has yours. I cannot refuse any more than you can.'

'If you take me to the temple at dawn, when will I be thrust into the underworld?'

'At midnight. That is when the sacrifices happen.'

I'd been quickly plotting. 'I'll try to help you there, Slither. I am fighting a war on behalf of Pan and, in order to preserve myself and allies such as you, I must be ruthless. When it's time to be pushed through the portal into the underworld, I will strike. I will first free the other human prisoners. I don't think they'll have much chance of escaping Valkarky but it will cause a distraction. Then I'll kill as many of the priests as I can. I can't guarantee that none will escape, so I would advise you to leave Valkarky as soon as you've delivered me to the priests. You should be able to get well clear of the city before they can work out what's happened and pursue you.'

'I will do as you say, Wulf, and thank you for that. Now sleep and gather your strength for the ordeal that lies ahead of you. Who knows, maybe we shall meet again.' The Haizda mage nodded towards the spook's staff that was leaning against the wall of the small room. 'I will keep that with me and perhaps one day I will be able to return it.'

I shook my head and smiled. 'It is part of this tulpa. When I change form it vanishes with me. Didn't you notice that it had gone from the wall when I changed into the warrior?'

'I was too busy trying to save my poor servant from your sword, Wulf!' he said with a smile.

I was fascinated by Slither and sad our time as allies was so short. Who knew, as he said, if we would ever cross paths again.

The following morning, we set off for the temple having already said our goodbyes. I was inhabiting the tulpa of the boy, Wulf, dressed as a spook and with the chain round my neck still marking my lowly status within Valkarky as a human slave.

When we reached the entrance to the temple, Slither stepped forward and spoke to the two guards. I could not understand a word he said. He'd explained that both Kobalos and humans from the lands that bordered them spoke a language called Losta: I had read about this in Nicholas Browne's glossary.

Then Slither took the chain from my neck and tucked the length of it into the pocket in his long black coat. Finally, he walked away without meeting my gaze or speaking a word to me. One of the guards prodded me into the temple with his spear.

If this was the Temple of Golgoth it was far less than impressive. For one thing it was not adorned with statues or carvings – the walls were plain and the floor constructed of plain black tiles. But its shape was unusual. It was cylindrical although quite small, probably less than sixty feet in diameter, but that cylinder was very high and open to the sky.

How easy it would be to take the shape of the sky wolf and fly to freedom. But I was here on Pan's command to attempt to destroy Golgoth and I must endure whatever came first in order to have that opportunity. And Slither himself had risked too much for me to abandon him now.

Around the inside of the cylinder ran a spiral of narrow stone steps. I guessed that the portal was right at the top of the cylinder. The warriors pointed downwards, gesturing that I should sit upon the tiles and I immediately did so. There were three more Kobalos in the temple and tonsures were shaved into the crowns of their heads in a similar fashion to that of the monks at Kersal Abbey. These priests wore sabres at their belts and were dressed in long white robes that came almost down as far as the ground. One of the warriors with a spear remained within the room while the other went outside to guard the door.

It was a long weary wait, and nothing happened for hours. I was offered no food or water so I was glad of the breakfast that I had shared with Slither. Around noon, two more prisoners were brought into the temple and forced to sit close to me.

One of them spoke a couple of words to me but I didn't understand. They were probably speaking Losta. I shrugged and spoke back but they didn't understand me either. Then they started speaking to each other but only managed a few words before the Kobalos with the spear came across and made it clear that he wanted silence by jabbing one in the shoulder and drawing blood.

I hope to save you, I said to myself silently.

The hours passed very slowly and I watched the sky begin to darken overhead, wondering how long it was to midnight.

The three priests returned, paying us three prisoners no attention whatsoever and knelt facing each other and began to chant. I felt the air in the temple becoming much colder and suddenly snow started to fall. At first it melted quickly but soon covered the black tiles in a cold white carpet.

Then that white layer of snow began to change colour, gleaming with a hint of red. I looked up then and saw that the sky was red, a certain indication that I was gazing upwards at an underworld. But it was not the deep baleful red that I'd experienced previously. In the other underworlds I'd visited, the sky had always been clear although without stars. This was covered with heavy cloud which dulled the colour a little.

The priests came to their feet and gestured towards the spiral flight of steps. It must be midnight. We were about to be pushed up those stone steps and into Golgoth's underworld.

I hung back a little, allowing the two other human sacrifices to ascend the steps first. They would be safer up there when the fighting began.

I changed into the form of the warrior, called out 'Sword!', felt it drop into the scabbard and drew it quickly, gripping it in both hands ready to fight for my life. The four Kobalos froze only for a moment and then they attacked.

As usual, the warrior was fast and economical, each movement of my blade a killing stroke. The fifth Kobalos warrior, the second guard with a spear, was the last to die. He had heard the commotion and run into the temple and straight onto my sword. They were all dead. By now Slither should be well clear of Valkarky. Now there would be nobody to report the part that he had played here.

I gripped the two human prisoners by their arms and dragged them from the steps towards the door of the temple and thrust them through. 'Run! Run!' I cried. Of course, they didn't understand my words but I made myself clear with gestures and, whether they understood me or not, they ran off into the night. I didn't give much for their chances of escaping but I certainly thought they'd be better off than as sacrifices in Golgoth's underworld.

That done, I returned the sword to the scabbard then began to sprint up the spiral of steps towards the portal at the top of the temple. I reached the top and emerged into a frozen forest, the trees laden with ice and snow and bowed low under the weight.

I glanced about me but there was nobody there. I'd expected servants of Golgoth to be waiting to seize any human sacrifices, meaning I'd have to fight again. Quickly I changed my form, becoming the wolf tulpa, Black Fang, and ran off into the forest. I realized that the further I ran it was likely that the wolf would have difficulty in finding the way back to the temple. But Piddle and his incredibly sensitive nose would certainly be able to follow Black Fang's route back to its source.

And what of Golgoth? Was he somewhere within this underworld or located elsewhere within the dark?

I'd read the accounts from Tom Ward's notebooks and they gave no clear picture of the Old God. All Tom had reported was that he'd spoken in a deep voice, and as he approached there was a grinding and rumbling noise as if he were forcing his way up through rocks and rubble to reach the surface of the world. Once there, he was enclosed by darkness with just his huge red eyes gazing out of it.

So I had no indication of his true appearance. No matter – no doubt I would find out soon enough.

I continued to lope through the trees. I had a feeling that this underworld was vast, far larger than the others I'd visited previously. I paused from time to time and listened but there was absolute silence as if I were the only living entity in this place.

Then, the third time I came to a brief halt, I heard it – a distant horn. Then came the faint baying of hounds and I knew one thing beyond the shadow of a doubt. Hunters.

And I was the prey.

21

THE RETURN OF THE PIPER

I ran faster, wondering how far they were behind me.

The horn sounded again and then the clamour of the hounds became louder. They were closing fast. The ground had been flat so far but now I reached the foot of a steep treeless slope and bounded up it as speedily as I could. I was tempted to change into the sky wolf and attack my pursuers, make *them* flee instead of me, but instinct told me it would be the wrong thing to do. I should hide my capabilities for a time when I really needed them.

When I reached the summit of the slope I paused briefly and glanced backwards. There were about a dozen hounds and three riders close behind – riders that were not human but green-scaled demons with antler horns growing out of their foreheads.

As was usually the case, one hound was in the lead – it would be the largest and fastest of the pack. I bounded down the slope and into the trees and began to slow my pace a little. I could hear the leading hound getting closer. It would be too far ahead of the others for it to get any help. I'd have to finish it quickly.

I glanced back again as it closed with me. Its fur was as black as mine but its head and jaws were exceptionally large. As I turned to face the creature, it leaped towards me. I twisted away before its jaws touched me and in a second I had reversed that movement and ripped out its throat to leave its body twitching and bleeding into the snow.

Then I ran on into the trees. It wasn't long before a second hound began to close in on me. I wished at that moment that I had my grey wolf tulpas at my side. We would make short work of this whole pack. I killed the second hound just as easily as the first but now three more of them were boxing me in, and they would not be so easy.

I changed my shape, driven to it at last, becoming the sky wolf, but very small indeed, no larger than a midge that hovers in a swarm over water in the County summer. I flew up into the branches and escaped the attention of the hounds.

The three demons rode into the area below me and began to circle, studying my tracks in the snow. I had killed two of their hounds and eluded them, but in doing so I had now alerted them to the fact that I was no ordinary prey, not the usual sacrifice that the Kobalos priests cast into this icy underworld.

After a while they rode away, their hounds following, but I stayed exactly where I was for a long time. How had they discovered my position in the first place? Had the hounds sniffed my scent even at a great distance? It was too dangerous to take on the shape of Black Fang again so I made myself slightly larger and flew on in the direction I'd originally taken.

Something began to concern me. I'd seen no other creatures in this frozen underworld forest. Soon I would need to eat or my strength would start to decline. In the shape of Black Fang, I could go back and devour the flesh of the hounds that I had slain, but the demons and surviving dogs might be hiding nearby. I didn't want to fall into a trap.

I flew on, astonished at the incredible size of this underworld. It seemed without end. Then my heart leaped! I heard a noise ahead – the music of pipes. Could it be Pan? How much better my chances would be if he had joined me here to directly align his strength with mine. But then I realized that the music was slightly different and that I had heard it before.

I came to a clearing among the trees. At its centre was a small lake, the sheet of ice that had covered it now broken into fragments and floating on the water which reflected the red of the sky. To one side was a large log and a man with a pointy hat was sitting on it eating food from a large basket.

It was not Pan. It was the Piper.

Obviously he must have emerged from the water, but his clothes were dry. He patted the log, indicating that I should sit beside him, and I became the boy Wulf and accepted his invitation after first resting my staff against the trunk of the nearest tree.

'You are hungry, Wulf. Please eat your fill!'

I was ravenous and didn't need to be asked twice. Within the large basket were bread, thick slices of ham, plump tomatoes and a variety of cheeses. Unfortunately, there was no crumbly County cheese, something which, like most spooks, I'd acquired a taste for but I didn't complain and began to eat.

'Eat as much as you can – it's vital that you keep up your strength – you will find no food in this frozen wasteland that Golgoth calls home.'

'Then what does Golgoth feed upon?' I asked, knowing that even a god required sustenance.

'He devours his servants and they, in turn, feed upon the human sacrifices,' said the Piper, biting off a large mouthful of bread.

I thanked him for both the food and the information, and we dined in silence for a while, eating ravenously.

'I am here to warn you, Wulf. Golgoth and his servants know that you are here. You have lost the element of surprise so go back the way that you came and escape into Valkarky before taking to the skies. Better to leave now and live to fight another day – that is my advice.'

'Pan asked me to slay Golgoth. I can't leave without at least attempting to do that.' I knew the god would be displeased if I didn't.

The Piper shook his head. 'You have no chance of surviving for long here. Golgoth has hordes of servants within this cold underworld and many will be dangerous and powerful adversaries in their own right. They're searching for you even as I speak. As for Pan, although he loves living creatures, individuals are not important to him. He would allow you to die without a moment's regret.' I knew this to be true. But Pan and I needed each other. I hoped that, for now, that would be enough.

'And if I disobey him and don't even try to destroy Golgoth?'

'He will not be pleased – I think we can certainly be sure of that. But he knows your worth and how successful you've been fighting a war against elements of the dark on his behalf. So, in time you will be forgiven.'

I nodded but was resolute. 'I can't turn back yet. Do you know where Golgoth is to be found?'

The Piper pointed into the trees, not too far from the direction in which I'd already been travelling. 'You will reach his dwelling soon. It is extremely large – you can't miss it.'

'So I thank you for your warning and advice – and also for the food – but I must go on. I can't give up so easily.'

'I thought that would be your reply. You should also know that the seeds that are one of your gifts from Pan will work again now his power is restored. You might find them very useful here.'

'I thank you,' I said with a smile. It was good to have the seeds at my disposal again but I had no idea how they could be deployed effectively against the Lord of Winter.

'Here is something else that might also prove useful. It is your favourite food! I'm afraid that there's not much of it but it will sustain you when you need your strength the most! Save it for a moment of extreme danger.'

He handed me a small paper bag. It was blue and twisted at the top to close it. I grinned at him. It would contain crumbly County cheese. I pushed it into the pocket of my gown and came to my feet. Without saying goodbye, the Piper turned his back on me and, carrying the basket under his arm, walked into the water. The tip of his pointy hat was the last thing to disappear from view.

I picked up my staff and headed in the direction that he'd indicated, suddenly wishing that I'd asked about Jenny and whether she was reunited with her people. But I couldn't dwell on that too long. I needed to press on. My boots were leaving prints in the snow that would be easy to follow but I knew that if any pursuers came close I could soon take to the sky. Besides, Golgoth's dwelling was very near now and no doubt I was travelling towards his demonic servants. The danger lay ahead, not behind.

I crested a hill and there it was, standing at the centre of a huge clearing in the forest.

I was astonished. I'd seen other dwellings set within underworlds: the strangely warped stone house within the stone circle near Keswick in Cumbria; the Temple of Circe with its colonnade of pillars in the style of Greece; and the home of Hrothgar, a mansion with tall windows but only one floor designed to accommodate the tall thin giant.

But this was on another scale altogether.

For one thing it was incredibly high with battlements and a large tower positioned at each corner, but its breadth was astonishing too. The largest castle I'd ever seen was the one at Caster but four of them would have easily fitted within the walls of Golgoth's massive citadel. It gleamed a reflected red from the sky and I could see that it had been constructed from huge blocks of ice. All that was but for the entrance.

I studied it carefully. There was no sign of movement either within or around its massive walls. No sounds carried towards me. The citadel seemed to be deserted, the huge wooden double doors wide open and a heavy iron portcullis raised. It was almost as if I was being invited to enter – and I knew that it was a trap.

So intent was I in studying that colossal citadel of ice that I was not aware enough of danger or when the trap would take place.

The attack took me completely by surprise.

22

THE MAGIC OF LOKI

There was no horn piercing the silence, no baying of hounds – just three demons riding to attack, their black antler horns stark against the baleful red sky. They wore curved blades at their belts, but instead of spears the three wielded long black chains with heavy orbs attached to the ends. They whirled them about their heads and I saw their intention was to cast their chains at me, body-binding me and making me immobile.

The first rider cast his chain, but I stepped nimbly to the left and it fell harmlessly into the snow. He drew his sword and charged at me.

I was dressed and armed as a spook and did not have the sword and mail armour of the warrior. But a spook could fight and, wielded with skill, his staff could be deadly. I released the silver-alloy blade so that it gleamed like red fire and thrust the rowan staff upwards as the demon charged towards me. The blade pierced his side and he shrieked and fell into the snow, staining it redder than the sky.

The second demon was on me before I could react and this time his chains did not miss their target. They wrapped round my legs, spinning me so I fell hard onto the snowy ground, the breath driven from my body. The two demons leaped from their horses, gripping their swords, and I tried to roll away from them, feeling certain that they intended to kill me.

I tried to change into the sky wolf but nothing happened. Then I tried to become the warrior with exactly the same result. My blood ran cold. Just as when I was captured near the castle and the metal band that bound my wrists had prevented me from shifting my shape, the same was happening now. Then it had been the magic of Loki. Was this his magic too?

But instead of slaying me where I lay, all they did was stare down at me before sheathing their weapons. One of them picked up my staff and with a contemptuous grunt snapped it into two pieces and threw it away. I felt the loss of it like a pain. Then they attached a longer chain to the one already binding my legs and connected it to the saddle of one of their horses.

Without further ado they began to ride down towards the castle, dragging me behind them. At first it was hardly a trot but gradually they speeded up. Had it been grass or hard ground below me my clothes would have been ripped from my back and my skin lacerated and flayed by the friction. But the snow was deep and that took away the worst of it, although I was still bumped about, my head hitting the hard floor and taking the breath out of me. I assumed I was about to meet Golgoth.

When we reached the entrance of the citadel, they slowed right down, riding under the portcullis at a sedate pace. We were now in a very large courtyard open to the red sky, the surface paved with bricks of ice and there – right at its centre – I saw what at first glance I took to be a gallows.

Was I to be hanged? I spotted that a chain hung from it, at the end of which was a metal cage, large enough to contain at least one person. Below it was a shaft leading down into darkness. Then, behind us, the portcullis clanged down into place, closing off the entrance, and I heard a wild shrieking from above.

I looked up to see hundreds of creatures descending the walls, leaping from ledge to ledge. They looked like large hairy apes but had long snouts with fanged jaws. They reached the ground and raced towards me, gibbering and salivating as if with hunger.

Was I to be devoured alive?

But rather than eat me they seized me and two of them gripped the chain that bound my legs and dragged me across the ice towards the metal cage. The others circled at a distance, filling the air with their wild savage cries. When we reached the cage, they opened the door and pushed me inside before slamming it closed and locking it.

Then there was a grinding and clanking of chains and the cage shuddered like a live thing and then began to descend very slowly, carrying me down into the darkness below the citadel.

I looked up, wondering if that would be my last ever glimpse of the sky, and then smiled grimly to myself for this was not the true sky but the upper limit of an Old God's underworld. How I wished that I was back in the County, not here having been sent on this doomed mission by Pan who cared nothing for individuals. I was only a small player, a pawn on a chessboard, and I was about to be sacrificed.

Down went the cage ever deeper into the darkness. Had I been in the shape of the sky wolf or even Black Fang, I would have been able to see my surroundings far more clearly, but the boy Wulf had ordinary human vision and could see nothing but blackness. I could, however, sense the walls of the shaft just inches from the limits of the cage, which seemed to be increasing in speed as it plummeted downwards.

At last, I felt it begin to slow and there was a sudden jar that shook the whole cage as it finally came to a halt. Here there was a little light – a torch on a bracket in the far corner of what appeared to be a large cellar. I waited a few minutes to allow my eyes to adjust to the gloom, then looked at the chains which bound my legs.

If I could release myself, I would be free of their power which prevented me from shifting my shape. Without that, I had no faith that I could defeat and destroy Golgoth. All I wanted now was to take to the air and escape as the Piper had advised.

I'd been lying on my side but now pulled myself up into a sitting position to examine my bindings. But when I studied the chains, my heart sank further. There was dark magic involved. The chains had fused together as if they had been beaten on a blacksmith's anvil. There was no way that I could separate them and free myself. My situation seemed hopeless.

Then there was a rumbling and a grinding from deep below the cellar where the cage now rested. It sounded like some huge beast was thrusting its way upwards, pushing aside rock to clear a path. And the terror grew rapidly within me as I recalled the accounts of Tom Ward where he'd described exactly that same sound as Golgoth forced his way to the surface up on Anglezarke Moor.

The ominous rumbling grew louder and the whole cellar began to shake as if in the throes of an earthquake, the cage rocking from side to side, threatening to topple over.

And suddenly Golgoth was present in the cellar. At first, I couldn't see him – but I sensed his malevolent presence and felt the temperature drop alarmingly.

He was in the farthest corner from the flickering torch, and gradually I began to see something of his appearance. He was a dark shapeless mass from which two huge red eyes glared in my direction. He was indistinct, and I thought I could see limbs but, if so, there were a lot of them and they writhed like snakes.

When Golgoth finally spoke to me, his voice was deep and thunderous.

'What a fool you are, human! What hubris! What presumption! You thought you could enter my lair and slay me. Now, to your cost, you know how hopeless your mission was. You will pay in pain for your folly!'

I seized the bars and dragged myself to my feet, not wishing to be attacked while I was lying down. I would have pride in my death at least. I saw jagged streaks of white on the ground radiating outwards from Golgoth and racing towards me. When they reached the cage, I saw that it was frost. The bars became white and were suddenly so cold that pain shot through my hands and up both arms. My hands stuck to the frozen bars and I managed to pull them away just in time, falling back onto the floor of the cage.

The extreme cold gripped me from head to foot but I felt that it was worse in my left hand. I held it up before my face and saw that it was white with frost. The sharp pain in it increased.

'*That is merely a taste of what lies ahead of you, human,*' Golgoth roared. '*I could freeze your whole body into a block of ice that would shatter into pieces as you fell. But that would be too easy a death. Each time I visit you I will take a small piece of your body. Perhaps a finger, or maybe I should start with your nose. You will live in pain here for many long weeks. Each piece of you that I freeze will add to your torment. Think upon that.*'

Then suddenly Golgoth was gone. The air instantly became warmer and there were no red eyes glaring at me from the darkness. I tried to examine my hand but the light from the distant flickering torch made it difficult.

Had he already destroyed my left hand? The pain had lessened but it felt totally numb. I knew that extreme low temperatures could cause frostbite. The circulation of the blood ceased and the flesh blackened and died. Some said that a dead finger could be snapped off like a blackened twig.

What had he done to me?

23

CHINESE BOXES

The numbness gradually eased, to be replaced by fresh pain as the circulation of my blood was gradually restored. I rubbed it with my right hand to speed up that process and within ten minutes, to my relief, knew that my hand would recover.

But what about the next time? Golgoth had warned that he would visit me again.

I made myself as comfortable as possible on the floor of the cage, trying not to think about what lay ahead of me. I had not expected to die slowly, to be tortured. I had believed that I would die a bloody but swift death fighting this powerful assailant from the dark. I hadn't even got to fight.

Some think that when you die your whole life flashes before your eyes. Whether or not that is true I neither knew nor cared but I certainly began to review the things that had happened to me that brought me to this place.

As a child I'd had nightmares so bad that both my mother and I thought that I was being visited by a demon. So, she'd sent me to Kersal Abbey where I'd become a noviciate monk and been surrounded by holy people and protected by their prayers. Sent by the Abbot to work for a local spook called Johnson and secretly spy on him, I'd gradually entered the world of spooks and met Tom Ward and his wife, Alice. And then, of course, Tilda . . . But the direction of my life had suddenly changed when rather than continuing as a spook's apprentice I'd encountered Hrothgar and discovered my true abilities and vocation – to become a tulpar and creator of wraiths and gristles, different types of tulpa.

The big decision that changed my life and brought me to this cage – and a slow and painful death – had been my decision to fight the dark. Hrothgar had been a scholar, gathering information as part of his love of learning. I had decided to continue as a spook, bringing to the job my own special gifts. I had chosen to become like Tom Ward, a hunter of the dark. After that I'd finally aligned myself with the Old God Pan, fighting a war against the dark on his behalf. Grimalkin, Thorne and Jenny had all been loyal and strong allies. I was thankful to them all.

But I had lost and now even Pan couldn't help me.

Suddenly, despite everything that I faced, I felt a sudden surge of hunger and remembered the food that the Piper had given to me. I hoped that it was good County cheese. I deserved something nice as I looked death in the face. I reached into the pocket of my gown and pulled out the small blue paper parcel that contained it. I noticed how small it was. It was hardly large enough to take even the edge off my hunger.

But when I twisted the bag open there was another one inside – this time it was coloured red. Amused, I twisted that open too. Within was another bag – this time it was yellow. My amusement faded. Each bag was smaller than the previous one. This was a real disappointment and my hunger increased.

Five minutes earlier I had faced torture and death and that had naturally taken away my appetite. So why was I suddenly so ravenous and being mocked by smaller and smaller paper bags, each one likely to contain less food?

It was like Chinese boxes. Part of Kersal Abbey's income had come from copying illuminated manuscripts for the libraries of titled wealthy men. Then a very lucrative special commission had been received. This was to copy a sequence of seven Chinese boxes, each one smaller than its predecessor, that would fit together.

One of the monks had been a very talented carpenter and he had been given the job by the Abbot. He'd protested that he lacked the necessary skills and materials to do the job but his protests had been over-ruled. I saw what he finally crafted. The boxes fitted tightly together, one inside the other. They were a good copy of the originals with a few minor changes to the gold and silver inlays that decorated each box.

The commissioner refused the boxes on the grounds that they were not sufficiently accurate copies. The poor carpenter was then punished by the Abbot. He had to survive on one serving of bread and water a day for sixty days and spend three extra hours every day on his knees.

I remember being really angry at the injustice of that and had felt sorry for the poor monk. But now I felt sorry for myself. I'd reached the seventh and final paper bag which was green. It was so small that surely it could hardly contain even the smallest portion of cheese. I must have fallen for a ruse by the Piper.

By now my hunger was raging and I untwisted that bag and peered inside. It was as I feared. All it contained was the tiniest piece of white crumbly County cheese, hardly larger than a few grains of sand.

But I still wanted to eat it – I was desperate to get it into my mouth and off that green paper where it was gleaming like a star. Afraid that I might drop it if I tried to lift it out with my fingers, I put the tip of my tongue into the bag, drew the minuscule morsel back into my mouth and swallowed it.

My breath stopped. My heart thudded painfully. I felt an instant flare of energy. The pain increased and I convulsed, feeling that my body was being torn apart. Then I came straight to my feet. How that happened I didn't know. Earlier

I'd had to pull myself upright by gripping the bars of the cage.

The chains fell from my legs and clanged down onto the floor of the metal cage. I was free! The cheese had been imbued with magic! It wasn't a ruse, but help exactly when I'd needed it the most.

Then I realized that as I was free of those chains I could well be free of the constricting magic that they had exerted. A second later, that proved to be true.

I became Saint Quentin and it took him but a couple of seconds to undo the lock and open the door of the cage. I changed again, this time to the warrior tulpa, and walked outside to gaze at the dark corner where Golgoth had materialized. There was no sign that he had ever been there.

I looked up. The cellar was very deep but I could just about see a small square of red above, the sky of Golgoth's underworld.

The sensible thing was to change into the sky wolf and escape while I could. Hadn't the Piper intended me to do that? Wasn't that why he'd provided the magic that freed me from my shackles? Almost certainly, I thought, because he had counselled me to escape before I reached the citadel. But something stubborn within me had resisted that. And still did.

I went over the conversations that I'd had with Slither. We'd discussed what new wraith I could create that might have some chance, however slight, of defeating Golgoth. But despite bringing my imagination to bear upon the problem, I had arrived at no solution. He could freeze and shatter anything that moved and breathed. Slither spoke of a frog he had seen revived after being frozen solid on the borders of his lands, but even that would not avail. I would be vulnerable and shattered by Golgoth at will.

Yet even if I had a clear idea about what to create, now I had insufficient time. Golgoth might return at any minute.

There had to be some other way . . .

I was standing outside the cage, leaning back against its closed door, when I heard the first rumble from deep below the ground. Golgoth was on his way back.

I suddenly remembered something else the Piper had said to me.

'Seeds!' I cried, and they filled my mouth, saturating it with bitterness.

'Sword!' I shouted, and there was the usual pleasing rasp as it slid into the scabbard upon my back.

'Thorne!' I cried finally, more in hope than anticipation of a response. There was no silver sphere, no grinning girl bristling with blades to help me in my fight against Golgoth. I could only assume that Grimalkin and Thorne had not yet found and seized the cauldron. But her name suddenly became an inspiration to me as I considered how I might defeat Golgoth.

The rumbling increased in volume and the temperature started to drop. Golgoth materialized in the same corner as before, his malevolent red eyes glaring at me from the darkness.

'*A fool you be but you never fail to surprise me, human,*' Golgoth said. '*You are no longer bound but that will avail you nothing. I will start your suffering by removing your nose.*'

As jagged lines of frost raced towards me, I spat my mouthful of seeds onto the cellar floor. Then I shaped their growth with my imagination. Green shoots sprang upwards at an astonishing speed.

I created a wall of green thorns between me and the approaching frost. It was exactly what I'd intended to do.

They withered and died, touched by the extreme cold. But I made more, replacing them quickly. The new ones quickly shrivelled too. As they died, I felt a blast of cold in my face but a third spurt of green growth erupted and this time I positioned it a few steps closer to Golgoth. I had also made the green barrier twice as thick.

I stepped forward through the dying thorns as a fresh green barrier was bursting upwards even nearer to the Lord of Winter.

'*Fool! Do you think that a few weeds can save you from my icy blast? All you gain is a little time!*'

I didn't waste my breath bothering to reply. I repeated the process and now I was almost within striking range of my enemy. But I had a sudden scare. Rather than withering the whole wall of greenery, Golgoth did something unexpected.

Instead of a general blast of cold, he sent an icy spear towards me which burned a circular hole through the thorns and seared the edge of my left shoulder just as I stepped sideways rapidly to avoid the full force of the attack. The pain was sharp and the intense cold felt like burning but I didn't think any serious damage to my body had been done. The small portion of the ice-cold spear that struck me had been deflected by the warrior's chain-mail armour.

Now I came to the moment of truth. This was the risky bit. The moment that I parted the curtain of thorns to strike at Golgoth, he would attack me with another deadly ice-spear. How good was my control over the thorns? Just as a spook routinely practises casting his silver chain, before that early winter came to the County I had practised with the thorns back in Chipenden. But I should have worked at it harder. How I wished I had put more time and effort into developing my skills when using Pan's gift.

A fresh barrier of thorns sprouted to form a green shield and then I parted it with a wish, so that a very narrow gap in that defensive curtain remained open for less than a second. But it was enough time and I struck through it at Golgoth with my sword, feeling the edge of the blade bite.

The god screamed and I knew that I had hurt him. But how fast would he recover? How quickly could he regenerate after being wounded?

The whole barrier shrivelled but I replaced it faster than it died. Now I tried something else. Concentrating even harder, I used my imagination to control the thorns. I hadn't only created a green wall sprouting from the ground between us, I added an extra point of growth – this one from directly below Golgoth where he squatted in the dark corner of the cellar.

I parted the curtain and saw how the thorns began to wrap themselves round him but, frustrated, saw that they died quickly at each contact with his body. I sliced downwards with my sword again. The first time I'd cut him, my target had been his head. But I'd glimpsed myriad limbs attached to his body. They resembled writhing tentacles and my sword now severed two of these. The thorns that were still erupting wrapped themselves around the two severed appendages and pulled them down into the earthen floor of the cellar.

Now I knew how I could win against the god. I needed to dismember him and have him carried off by the thorns into different underground locations. That should make it impossible for Golgoth to reassemble himself.

So I set to work using all the speed, precision and economy of movement that the warrior was capable of. Even so, there were moments of great danger when I slightly misjudged the timing or the immediate threat. At one point an icy blast almost removed my head from my shoulders but, bit by bit, I cut Golgoth into pieces and the green thorns, twisting like snakes, carried them away deep into the ground.

He roared with frustration. *'You will not be victorious, you insignificant human,'* he shouted in anger.

I said nothing in response but dug in, methodical and steadily creating and chopping. And finally the right angle came for me to take his head. He saw it coming and so as my sword severed his neck, it did so with his mouth in a wide-open O of anger.

But still there were limbs and the rest of his body. I could not relax.

How long this battle persisted it was impossible to know, but I fought on, striking again and again at my enemy.

And then at last it was over.

I felt completely numb. Spent. Had I truly won? If I had truly won this battle in the cellar, Golgoth would pose no threat for a long time.

24

A HOWL OF TRIUMPH

Now I had to make my escape, so with what felt like my last remaining bit of energy I changed into the sky wolf and flew up the shaft towards the red sky of the underworld far above. Would Golgoth's servants know what had happened to him? Would they be gathered above ready to take their revenge?

But the huge courtyard was deserted, the atmosphere different somehow. There would be another portal that led straight into Hell. Had they left for their true home knowing that this underworld would eventually cease to exist? Hrothgar's had not long survived his death. With his power withdrawn from maintaining its existence, the same would be true of Golgoth's also, I assumed. Eventually it would become a part of the human world again.

I soared over the high walls of the citadel and headed in the approximate direction that should take me to the portal back into Valkarky. After flying for about half a minute or so, I landed on the snowy ground and changed into Piddle. Quickly, I took my bearings to find that I wasn't too far off course but Piddle gave me a precise direction.

Back in the air, within moments I flew over the pond where I had met the Piper. But for that meeting with him, I would be being tortured, with more of it to come and my painful death somewhere in the future. I owed him a lot. I wondered if I would be called upon to repay the debt.

I also wondered about Valkarky. I knew I would have to wait for the portal to re-open. Would priests and Kobalos guards be waiting in ambush there? Would they know what had happened to their god, Golgoth?

The only other means of escape would be to find and use the portal to Hell. But I'd be alone there and in great danger. Time might move at a faster or slower rate than it did back on earth. I thrust that worry to the back of my mind. That was also true of an underworld – who could know how long had passed here? I could do nothing about it so I decided that I needed to concentrate on getting back into the Kobalos city and then escaping from there.

The portal was closed as I'd expected. There was a large opaque circle in the snow below me. I knew that when it was opened it would become clear. So I settled down close to that entrance and waited.

A Howl of Triumph

There was no way to measure the passage of time and the wait seemed interminable. Just as I thought I might pass out with sleep and hunger, the portal began to clear and three humans were pushed upwards, jabbed by the spears of their Kobalos captors and forced onto the snow. It was clearly time for the next batch of sacrifices.

Well, they would not be tortured or eaten this time, but the underworld was desolate and there was no food to sustain them. Eventually they would starve. With ease I could have rescued them and led them back down into the city. But that would only have been the first step, and any attempt to free them from the city would have been doomed to failure. There were thousands upon thousands of Kobalos warriors and there was no hope of fighting our way to freedom. It hurt to leave them to their deaths but I could do nothing. I would return to the County and continue in my quest to help people there.

I made myself very small and flew down the shaft into the temple, undetected even by the guards at the gate. Once within the city, I flew at speed towards the entrance. But I should have known that it would not be that easy. The Kobalos had many mages skilled in the use of dark magic.

I saw winged creatures flying up to intercept me, so increased my size to defend myself against their attack. They looked clumsy with long bodies and very small stubby wings. As they drew nearer they reminded me of winged leeches and I could see blood smeared round their mouths. There were about a score of them and I saw no profit in fighting an aerial battle.

But they engaged me. The leader spat a globule of green slime straight at my head and I was very lucky to avoid it. No doubt the substance was some type of poison. I paid the creature back for that, raking its belly with my talons.

I was approaching the gate of the city and heard Kashilowa roar out a challenge. Somehow the gatekeeper knew of my approach. It was atop the wall close to the gate and I flew straight towards it gathering speed, my anger growing. The sky wolf wanted to drive it from the wall and kill it. But Kashilowa wanted to kill me too. It reared up its enormous head with its fanged jaws, drawing closer by the second, hundreds of its taloned legs writhing to rip me to shreds.

The human part of me overruled the sky wolf. After all, it was just a creature that had served the Kobalos, created by dark magic to do their bidding. And even the Kobalos were not my enemies. I had visited Valkarky to achieve the death of Golgoth and had succeeded. Let that suffice.

At the very last moment I changed the incline of my attack and passed over Kashilowa without harming it. As I flew on, I allowed myself to feel exultant, glorying in what I'd achieved, and I gave a loud howl of triumph far louder than the previous roar of the gatekeeper. That cry, the howl of the wolf, reverberated over the city. They would not soon forget my visit!

Then I was flying over the new walls which were still under construction and I was soon beyond Valkarky, a heavy grey sky overhead full of snow. As I flew, I put my pride aside – the monks at Kersal Abbey had always said it was the worst of the sins. I had achieved much but I had certainly not done it alone. And once more I thought of those who had helped me fight this long war. When my thoughts landed on Slither I wondered if he had made his escape. I would check to see if he was all right. That was the least that I could do. So, I flew south, heading for his ghanbala tree. It had been about a week's journey on foot from Slither's home to Valkarky. My speed was far in excess of that and I expected to overtake him within the hour.

Close to the ancient tree that was Slither's home, I flew lower. I saw prints in the snow made by heavy boots. They circled the tree. Then beyond them were the deeper indentations of hooves – maybe nine or ten mounted Kobalos who were heading in a southerly direction. I sped up.

Not very long after, I flew over the body of a dead Kobalos warrior half-buried in the snow. That gave me hope. Slither had fought back and reduced the number of his pursuers at least by one.

The heavy snowfall worried me. Eventually, the tracks would be covered. But within moments, I had flown over two more Kobalos warrior bodies. They had died together, and their blood stained the snow a bright red. But according to my reading of the footprints, there had to be at least six or seven of Slither's enemies still alive. Had they overpowered him?

At last I caught up with them and saw I had no need to worry. Slither was cutting at his foes with deft slices from his sabre, swaying in his saddle on the black stallion as he did so.

I swooped and with my talons I savagely brought two of the Kobalos warriors from their horses. They were probably dead before they hit the ground. Slither grinned up at me and began to fight with renewed vigour. He slew one more warrior and I quickly despatched the other two.

Then I landed and became the warrior once more. I offered a hand to help him down.

'Little Wulf! I have much to thank you for. But first – you were successful in the underworld?'

I smiled. 'I believe I was. But I wanted to make sure you had reached home safely.'

'Almost,' Slither told me with a smile. 'The Kobalos worked out my involvement – as you see.' And he gestured to the bodies around us.

'How long is it since you left Valkarky?' I asked.

'Just over a month,' he replied

'For me, time passed differently,' I told him. 'I spent no more than a day within that underworld.'

'You have experienced such things before, Little Wulf. We are all time travellers but, because of your visits to underworlds and the dark, you have done it far faster than most beings. And I must congratulate you, Wulf. It was a great and courageous achievement to slay Golgoth.'

'Could you tell at the time?' I asked.

'About two weeks ago there was a very small subtle change in the weather. Something that could only have happened if Golgoth was dead. At first it was hardly noticeable even when using my strongest magic. But the process is accelerating and soon everybody will see it.'

'It was tough. Perhaps one day when we are both rested, I'll give you a full account of how Golgoth died.'

'Why not stay now and I can give you food and rest?' Slither graciously offered, gesturing back in the direction of his tree.

But I declined – politely, of course. 'Thank you, but no. Now I'd like to get back to the County.'

'But will you be safe there? Loki will know what you have done and he may seek revenge. You are welcome to stay with me for as long as you want.'

I shook my head. 'I have to go back. I'm a spook and it's my duty to help to keep the County safe from the dark.' Privately, I also admitted to myself that I wanted to see both Grimalkin and Thorne again soon, and to discover what my friend Jenny was now up to.

'Then take care, my friend. Perhaps I will visit you next year. There is a portal between our land and Anglezarke Moor. During the war, it was used by Kobalos warriors to raid the County. It would have been too dangerous before because Golgoth could be summoned there. But I might be able to find a way to locate and use it.'

'You would be welcome,' I told him. And truly I meant it. There was much I would like to learn about this fascinating creature.

So I began the long journey back to the County. It was much easier this time. The weather was clear with a strong breeze but it was at my back and aided my flight rather than hindered it.

As I approached home, I had an irrational fear that the County would once more be in the grip of ice and snow – that the Trickster God would have already taken his revenge for what I had done. But I needn't have feared. As I entered the County border, we were in the heights of a glorious end of summer.

I paused just for a moment to feel the sun on my skin.

And then the Chipenden house came into view, and the howl of my wolves was there to greet me.

EPILOGUE

I rested for almost a week to fully regain my strength, then
once more I took up the routine role of the Chipenden spook.
The good weather persisted until the middle of October and
the County farmers had a late but very ample harvest. Nobody
would starve, thanks to Pan.

I had been home only briefly when a message appeared
on the mirror by the bedroom – written backwards as the
messages from Grimalkin had come to me most recently.

Wulf –

Congratulations on your victory. I have good news also.
We are closer than ever before to finding the crossroads and
the cauldron.
More soon
Grimalkin

This was good news – for that would not only give them the means to visit the earth after dark whenever they chose, but the magic of the cauldron would give them new strength to fight our future enemies.

Our most recent enemy, the Trickster God, had left me alone and that was something else to be grateful for.

At night, lying in bed in my room, the one used by dozens of spooks' apprentices over many generations, I sometimes became aware of the grandfather clock down in the library. I could hear its steady *tick-tock* and sometimes it seemed very loud, while at other moments it seemed to fade away almost to nothing. But still it was always there and for now the house remained safe.

One night I started to consider the comment that Slither had made – that we were all time travellers but that I travelled faster than most. But everyone was heading in the same direction – forward into the future. What if it were possible to go in the opposite direction? Go back to when Tilda was still alive and so were Tom, Alice and Spook Johnson?

It was not as crazy as it sounded. Underworlds could manipulate time – make it go faster or slower than it did in the outer world. Maybe somewhere there was an underworld that could send time into reverse?

But if I found such a place, would I make use of the chance to go back? It would mean leaving behind much of what I had accomplished. And I didn't think it was too prideful to reflect that I had accomplished a lot.

I was done. My war was over.

I was the last spook and now I would confine myself to my primary duty – defending the County.

It was enough.

A Note on This Book

This book was delivered in full only weeks before Joseph Delaney died.

He did not have the opportunity to work with his editors as he had on every other book, and so certainly there are some magical extra touches missing that would have emerged in the editing process.

Joe followed what he called 'the Bram Stoker method of writing', meaning he never plotted and instead discovered as he went. Joseph's family and Penguin Random House UK are confident that this book is published with Joe's blessing, so those extra 'discoveries' will have to exist in our imaginations – imaginations all the greater for the worlds and characters Joe created.

Over twenty years, Joe worked with so many people to bring his work to readers in countries across the globe.

Thank you to everyone who helped him to do this.

August 2023

'If you achieve all that I hope, then others will judge your life to have been worth living, son, even if you don't. You were born to serve the County. And that's what you've got to do.'
Mam, *The Spook's Secret*

JOSEPH DELANEY was the bestselling author of the Spook's series, which has been published in thirty countries and sold millions of copies. The first book, *The Spook's Apprentice*, was adapted into a major motion picture starring Jeff Bridges and Julianne Moore. Joseph passed away in August 2022, shortly after handing in his last manuscript.

IF YOU'D LIKE TO LEARN MORE ABOUT JOSEPH AND HIS BOOKS, VISIT:

www.josephdelaneyauthor.com

www.penguin.co.uk

THE SPOOK'S SERIES

WARNING:
NOT TO BE READ AFTER DARK

JOSEPH DELANEY

THE SPOOK'S

BLOOD

Stand against the dark — or lose everything . . .

JOSEPH DELANEY

THE SPOOK'S

SLITHER'S TALE

A new darkness is rising . . .

JOSEPH DELANEY

THE SPOOK'S

ALICE

Will old enemies take their deadly revenge?

JOSEPH DELANEY

THE SPOOK'S

REVENGE

Everything ends

JOSEPH DELANEY

THE SPOOK'S STORIES

WITCHES

Evil has many faces

THE SPOOK'S

BESTIARY

AS TOLD TO

JOSEPH DELANEY

JOSEPH DELANEY

SPOOK'S

A NEW DARKNESS

THE TIME HAS COME TO FIGHT ALONE

JOSEPH DELANEY

SPOOK'S

THE DARK ARMY

JOSEPH DELANEY

SPOOK'S

DARK ASSASSIN

DO YOU DARE ENTER
THE WORLD OF ...

WHEN LEIF'S FAMILY IS DESTROYED BY AN EVIL CREATURE,
BATTLE IS THE ONLY WAY TO GET REVENGE ...

READ JOSEPH DELANEY'S SPOOKY SERIES!

Crafty can't remember a time before the Shole –
a terrifying mist that will either kill you or
transform you into a terrifying monster,
known as an aberration. When Crafty is
recruited to join the Castle in the fight against
this evil, his life is changed forever . . .